DON'T PUSH ME

02. 26. 2021

B°A BOURNE

1

THANK YOU

To my Lord and Savior Jesus. I truly hope that I please Him in everything that I do.

To my wonderful wife Julia, my best friend and number one supporter who keeps everything 100 with me.

To my children Jada, Jasmyne, Davian and Janine who continue to make me a proud father.

To my Pastors Kevin and Pam Begley, who's sermon series "Silent No More" led me to write this book.

To Angel B, who blew my mind with the awesome book cover.

To Tameka Cozier for her time and wisdom in editing this project.

To Kells James and Francis McLean, who have supported me from day one with their valuable insight and taking time to read my drafts.

To Otis Morgan, Nicole Queensborough, Ken Goncalves, and Mindy Henry who have offered valuable advice or input for this project.

And last but not least, to my small yet growing reader fanbase who continue to encourage me every day!

Love and blessings, D.A

DISCLAIMER

The N-word is mentioned several times throughout the story. It is not used for entertainment purposes, but to describe the hate that takes place in today's society. It is not a reflection of the author's character. Thank you for understanding.

1

SKITTLES

I ask Annie multiple times if she's okay because she got struck by a smooth criminal.

On my way to my new job at Sutton Motors Assembly plant and I cannot stop smiling as I blast Michael Jackson's *Smooth Criminal* through the speakers. I am so excited! Not because this job required me to do a repetitive job on the assembly line, but I was getting more money than my previous job as a mechanic and a consistent paycheck!

Fixing cars is what I enjoyed the most from my former job. My former boss was a gambling addict and owed a bookie thousands of dollars. As a result, he gave pro bono repairs for the bookie's family, which meant he underpaid his mechanics. Getting paid for forty hours despite working fifty, was wearing me down very quickly. Thankfully, my childhood friend Simon told me to apply to Sutton Motors Assembly Plant for a production worker position and I did. Now after a week of classroom orientation, the real work was about to begin.

I'm singing the chorus as if I'm the late King of Pop. Those who know me realize that when I hear good music, I jam wherever I'm at, especially in my car. The subwoofers are kicking in my fully loaded 2009 Dodge Charger and I feel like I'm Michael Jackson with my long jet-black hair, minus the pale white skin. Thanks to my Black Trinidadian mother and Guyanese Indian father, my skin was a nice medium brown. Quite often I would get confused as someone from either India or Pakistan, but my roots are full West Indian.

There's something about Michael's music that makes me believe I'm on a stage in the Scotiabank Arena in Toronto, performing in front of thousands. I knew every lyric as if I wrote the track.

Suddenly, I notice another Dodge Charger behind me, a later model with lights on the roof. I make sure I'm driving under the speed limit, still singing the stanza.

I make a right turn. So does the police car. It doesn't stop me from singing the chorus. When I approach another traffic light I zoom through the yellow. The police car decided to stop at red. What a relief!

With joy I sing the chorus in full soprano mode!

Looking at the clock, it was 2:30pm. Two minutes away from work and I'll be fifty-eight minutes early. Lovely.

"OWWW!"

I shift into full jam mode for the rest of the song. When it finished, I tapped the song to repeat on my phone attached to the windshield. That's when I saw flashing lights in my rear view window. "You gotta be freaking kidding me," I grumbled as I pull my car to the side of the road. "I wasn't speeding. Lord, give me favor."

Rolling the window down, a frosty gush of wind slaps my face. The police officer looks inside and says, "I need to see your license, ownership and insurance sir."

I shook my head as I open the glove compartment. "May I ask why you pulled me over, officer?"

"You were using your phone while driving. Are you Edward Persaud?"

"Yes I am. Sir, the only thing I did was tap the screen to change a song. My phone stays in the holder while I'm- "

"One time is too much while driving."

This officer is lying. The cop was following me before I touched my phone, he just needed an excuse to pull me over. "Driving while black" is what it felt like and he's a white man built like Captain America.

Staring at the exterior he says, "Your windows look over-tinted."

"They shouldn't be," I answered. "I checked if the shade was legal before I put them on."

"You did it yourself?"

"Yeah I'm a mechanic."

"Are you heading to work now?"

"Yes."

"Where's your shop located?"

"I'm heading to Sutton Motors Assembly Plant."

"That's where you fix cars?"

"No sir. I build cars."

"I thought you said you're a mechanic."

"I am, I mean that's my- "

"You need to be truthful when I ask you questions, Mr. Persaud."

I literally bit my tongue to shut up. Everything that came out of my mouth was the truth, but this officer is looking to create drama and it's pissing me off. I just need him to leave so I can get to work.

The officer uses his flashlight to search the backseat. "What's with all the candy? Got the munchies?"

He was referring to the box of my nickname's sake. "I like Skittles."

"Do you smoke marijuana?"

"No."

"Do you smoke marijuana?"

"Wasn't I clear sir?"

"Answer the question again."

"No, I don't smoke marijuana."

"When's the last time you smoked marijuana?"

What the hell?

"Three months ago. Why? Isn't it legal now?"

"Not while driving. Do you mind stepping out the vehicle, sir?"

I snapped, "Yes I do mind, officer! It's freezing. Why can't you just gimme my ticket so I can go to work?"

"I need you to step out the car so I can search the vehicle. Pop your trunk please."

"Jesus take the wheel," I mumble while placing my hands on the roof of my Charger. The piercing cold on my fingertips feel like frostbite. In my defense, I thought I was only going from the parking lot to the plant, so I didn't carry a toque, scarf or gloves and now I'm paying the price. The officer is taking his sweet old time going through my deep trunk and under the car searching for weapons. It may have been only ten minutes, but the cold made it feel like an hour. It's embarrassing to stand outside my car looking like a criminal while people stare as they drive by, including my friend Audre who's heading to Sutton as well. Audree rolls down her window and shouts, "What the hell?" and continues driving while looking back. I can't even respond but I know a text is coming soon.

The officer approaches me and says, "OK, go back in your vehicle while I process your information. Give me a few moments."

"A few moments?" I cry. "For what? I gotta get to work!"

"What time do you start?"

"3:30."

"It's 2:45. Get in your car."

Anxiety is killing me as I wait in my Charger with the heater cranked to the highest temperature. Its 3:09pm, twenty-four minutes and counting since the cop went to his ride. I don't know the Sutton hotline number to call in sick or late- I didn't think I'd need it so early in my Sutton career. But I'm praying for God's favor that I make it to work on time and avoid a ticket, because this man doesn't have a reason to pull me over other than an ignorant suspicion.

I receive a text from Audre, who's already at work.

AUDRE
Why did you get pulled over???
ME
Idk. Driving while black?
AUDRE
SMFH...are u at work now?
ME
Nope
What's the work absence #?
AUDRE
Really? WTF...
1866-555-5550

A tap on the window. Finally, after twenty-nine minutes.

"Here you go, Mr. Persaud," the officer said, passing me my plastic. "I'm not giving you a ticket, just a warning. Hands off your phone while driving."

"So you needed to follow me for several blocks, search my car for weapons while I freeze outside, and then have me waiting for another half hour just to give me a warning?" I respond in frustration.

"You want a ticket? Give me another ten minutes and I'll gladly write you one," he answered with an attitude like he wants to hit me.

I shook my head. "Can I at least get your name?"

"You have fourteen minutes to get to work. If you speed, I'll stop you again."

I cuss him out after he walks away, and roll up my window. This nameless, arrogant SOB follows me the rest of my short journey, then zooms away when I turn into the parking lot of Sutton Motors Assembly. Walking as fast as I can, I scanned my card at 3:23pm, but it takes me six minutes to walk to the conference room where the new hires go on their first assembly day. There are no employees left, just a couple of people at a table.

"Sorry I'm late. I'm Edward Persaud," I said to the lady with the attendance sheet.

"Edward. We thought you quit," she grinned as she checks off my name. "Your supervisor was just here a few minutes ago."

The man next to her said, "I'll text Brad to come back."

"Thank you," I said. "I should've been here forty minutes ago but I was pulled over."

"It's okay. Sorry to hear that," she said. "Was it a big fine?"

"No fine."

"No fine? That's good, you should be happy."

The way I was treated? Hell no.

A short young man comes into the conference room looking frustrated. Dude looks like he just finished high school.

"Edward? I'm Brad, come with me."

As we walk down the aisle, Brad tells me that I would be working on the engine line. I grinned because I love working on engines, my favorite part of the vehicle. "Nice," I said.

Brad stares at me with curiosity. "You've worked on assembly before?"

"No, I'm a mechanic. Fixed hundreds of engines."

"Well, that means nothing now. Assembly is a whole new ball game buddy."

I disagree with his statement. Last week during orientation, the discussion leader told me that former mechanics who work on the assembly line have been excellent on their jobs. Brad sounds like another arrogant dude, like the nameless cop.

"Should I expect this from you on a regular basis?"

"Expect what?" I ask him, a bit confused.

"You showing up late. I don't wanna show disrespect, but every Black man that's been on my line lacked punctuality. Not saying that's you but...no offense."

As much as I want to respond to Brad's ignorance, I bite my tongue again. I don't need a second racial incident before the first hour of my first day.

<u>2</u>

<u>AUDRE</u>

It is 1:30pm on Monday afternoon and I'm running around the house like a mad woman. From the time I dropped my twin sons Terrell and Tristan to school, I went to the bank, bought groceries, cleaned the house, folded laundry and prepared dinner. Today is my first time working an afternoon shift, so this is a big transition for my family.

Thankfully my sons are sixteen so they don't need a sitter while I'm away. All Terrell and Tristan must do once they get home is eat dinner, clean the dishes and do their homework. They no longer have a father because my husband Hank died of pancreatic cancer two years ago. We both worked at an auto parts plant and it closed down a year before his death. Financially, it has been a rough two years- we downsized from a semi-detached home to renting a basement apartment. I did multiple jobs just to make a little over half of what Hank and I used to earn. Add that to the emotional distress of losing a husband and father, we needed some luck and the Sutton job couldn't come at a better time.

"Yes, the roast is done," I cheer after I hear the buzzer from the oven. I quickly put the clothes from the top washer to the lower dryer, which was also in the kitchen. Then, I took the dirty clothes from the laundry basket and placed them in the washer. That was followed by taking the roast beef out of the oven and carving it with an electric knife. It was a perfect medium rare. Tristan better not complain again about how tough the meat is. I shut off the boiling potatoes on the stove and began to mash them.

Once dinner is fully prepared, I pack some potatoes and veggies. No beef because I'm preparing myself to be a full-time vegetarian. I closed the Tupperware and placed it in my brand-new lunch bag that was large enough for my food, water bottle, paperback novel and an Essence magazine. Lastly, I double-check the front pocket to make sure my mints, plastic cutlery and tampons are there. Check. Time to go.

While I'm finishing up in the washroom, I hear the front door open. Why are my sons' home from school already?

Tristan, the youngest of the twins is taking a drink out of the fridge when I came out. "Hey luv. Where's your brother?"

"I left him in class," he answered. "I walked out and took the bus home."

"That's why you're home now? Why'd you leave class?"

"History teacher kept saying 'nigga' in class."

My eyes grow in shock. "Say WHAT? Is he Black?"

"Ma, you know I got no Black teachers. It was my White teacher Mr. Norris. Said it at least five or six times."

As much as I want to arrive to my first day at work early, I must hear this story from Tristan. The word nigger disgusts me, even when its only used by my Black people. I rebuked my brother at a BBQ for using the word in front of my sons when they were in Elementary school. So, with a few minutes to spare, I asked Tristan to explain the situation.

"So, Mr. Norris hands out suggestion papers wanting suggestions for a movie to watch during Black History month," he begins. "There were tons of good and bad selections as expected, but when a student suggested 'Boyz N The Hood', he got excited because it's his favorite Black movie. Suddenly Mr. Norris began talking like he was in a black barbershop, saying 'nigga' like it was part of his everyday vocab."

"Was he saying it directly at someone?"

"No, he was saying phrases like 'my nigga so and so', 'my nigga from back in the day'. He claims to have a lot of Black friends and he loves old school hip-hop like NWA and Tupac. So while he's speaking, my friend Jennifer who is Black asks 'How are you so comfortable saying nigga as a White person?' Mr. Norris says, 'I've always talked this way around my boys, I grew up in the hood. They used to call me White Chocolate. And they never minded me saying nigga because I always said nig-gah and not nig-ger. Ya feeling me?'"

My mouth is wide open. "This man really said that? Ohhh, I shoulda been in there-"

"That's exactly what I was thinking when Mr. Norris said this! You would've torn him apart. Anyway, so Jennifer then says 'Well, either way you say it that word offends me, and I've heard enough' and walks out of the classroom. I said, 'Me too' and followed her out a minute later."

I want to cry but I hold the tears. Tristan's stance makes me proud and thankful that he doesn't accept foolishness as a young Black teenager. I don't even need to call the school right now to complain because he stood up for himself.

"Good for her and good for you walking out on that foolishness," I say. "Did you report him to the Principal?"

"Jennifer was already there when I left class. We'll see what the school does about this."

"My question is why didn't Terrell follow you out? Didn't that conversation bother him enough to take a stand?"

Tristan shrugged his shoulders. "I think he was enjoying the discussion. Plus he has basketball practice after school."

"Oh yeah I forgot he told me that yesterday. Still, he should've walked out with you. That's the only time I suggest you leave class, when someone disrespects you or the color of your skin. Damn, you two are so different sometimes. Anyways, I'm off to work. Dinner's already prepared. Keep the house clean! And tell your brother to text me when he gets home."

"OK. Will you always be working evenings now?"

"No, just every two weeks. If I ever come home to a dirty house after work I will take away your phones. Got that?"

"OK. Bye Ma."

"Bye. Love you."

Driving to the Sutton Motors Assembly Plant, I'm feeling anxious about my first day on the assembly line. I'm so used to clerical and administrative work. As much as the orientation class was helpful the week before, I'm not sure how my body will react to repetitive physical work, two ten-minute breaks and a twenty-minute lunch. Shoot, my entire working career I had at least a forty-five-minute lunch. It's going to be an adjustment but I'm willing and determined to make this job work.

Two minutes away from the plant, I don't realize I'm speeding well over the limit until I see a police car a block ahead on the roadside. Slowing down, I notice a man with dark skin and long hair shivering outside in the cold while the cop searches his car.

"Why does that look like Skittles?" I say to myself out loud. Sure enough it's him because I recognize his Dodge Charger. "WHAT THE HELL?" I yell at the police officer after I scroll down the window. Obviously he pays me no mind, but Skittles saw me when I passed by.

I let out an F-bomb after I scroll up the front passenger window. Skittles and I have been friends for decades. He has the appearance of a gangster at times but he's a teddy bear. I'd never known Skittles to get in trouble with the law, so there was no doubt in my mind he was being racially profiled. Racially profiled and standing outside in freezing temperature when he should be at work on time.

After parking my car in the employee lot, I'm ready to text Skittles to ask him why he got pulled over, but not before texting my girl Tracey. I always told myself that whenever I saw a police officer it would be a reminder for me to give her a shout.

<u>3</u>

<u>TRACEY</u>

"Bill, I've been trying to get a hold of you," the man said as he approaches the older gentleman sitting in the diner.

"Brian!" Bill whispers, "I can't be seen with you. What the hell are you doing here?"

"The cops questioned me two days ago, asking me if I shipped child porn," Brian whispers back. "You never told me you make child porn videos man, what the f- "

"Shut up! You've seen the girls in the videos. They look mature, their body parts are quite developed, and they sound like they're over eighteen! I picked them good. Besides, the only way anyone would know that those immigrant whores were underage is if one of the girls said something."

"Man, I'm done if I go to jail because of this...you lied you sonofabitch! I'm not taking a fall for you-"

"Brian, I'm warning you now, if the cops find out I'm behind all this, I'm taking all of y'all done with me! That's a promise!"

"Sounds like a confession to me," I say to my partner Harpreet as I take off my headset.

"Let's go," Harpreet replies, as we run across the street into the diner.

"FREEZE! Halton Police!" I say as we approach the two men. "William O'Malley, you are under arrest for sex trafficking."

"DAMN YOU TO HELL!" Bill screams at Brian as he tries to swing a punch at him. Harpreet manages to grab his wrist and pull the senior's arm behind his back to handcuff him.

My expression is the usual stoic yet serious mode, while on the inside I'm overjoyed. I prayed for weeks that we would have enough evidence to arrest William O'Malley, a multi-millionaire investor who was operating an underground child pornography distribution. Brian is one of his distributors that agreed to work with us to avoid jail time, so we had him wired up and it worked. However, my guard must stay up. O'Malley has a sexist mindset and speaks with no filter, so I must be ready for whatever comes out of his mouth.

"You have the right to remain silent," I say. "Anything you say can be used against you in court. You have the right to-"

"PTOOOH!!!"

I stand in shock and rage as the man spits on my face.

"I don't speak to female niggers," William growls.

I was one step away from breaking his nose with my fist, when Harpreet does the honors and punches O'Malley across the jaw.

"You just added another few years to your sentence!" Harpreet says. "Let's go. I hope somebody caught your perverted ass on video!"

The waitress gives me a few napkins to wipe off the saliva, which is more than a few sprinkles. A part of me wants to vomit from the disgust. "Thank you," I say to her. "Where's your washroom? Can I use it please?"

"Absolutely, its across from the kitchen. I hope that old piece of crap dies in prison," she says in disgust.

Filling my hand with soap from the dispenser, I cover my entire face and scrub with a clean rag that the waitress kindly provided. Had to remove all my Mary Kay makeup that my friend Jessica hooked up for me. That prick's saliva got into my nostril and even in my mouth. It wasn't the first time getting spat at as a detective, but it's the first time in my face. This time it makes me question my career choice.

After a thorough face clean, I wash it for a second time because I feel so dirty. As a Black woman in the police force, I've been called 'nigger' numerous times by criminals, so my skin was quite thick. But spitting on someone is the ultimate disrespect, a slaveowner mentality and I'm not a damn slave. I am a proud wife, mother of twins and a new follower of Christ. But O'Malley made me feel like I lost my salvation.

"Lord, I know you said we need to love one another but I hate this man," I pray before leaving the washroom. "I know it's wrong, but I'm a work in progress. Give me wisdom on how to go about the rest of this day."

Harpreet decides to drive back to the station while I take shotgun. I really need a moment of downtime.

"Did I ever tell you how much I dislike Georgetown?" I ask.

"Every time we come," Harpreet grinned. "It figures that a racist scumbag like O'Malley lives here."

"My husband was born in Georgetown. His parents were forced to move when they received death threats because of their interracial marriage."

"Hmmm. Are we in Ontario or a small town in Mississippi?" Harpreet chuckles.

"I know right? Racism is everywhere in North America. That's why towns like this hate seeing an Indian and a Black detective, cuz they can't get away with their hate crimes. By the way, thank you for sucker punching that piece of sh- Lord help me. Thank you."

"I only responded the same way you would've reacted. That's why we work well together. Will you be okay questioning O'Malley?"

My flesh was more than ready- to rip him a new one.

"I don't know yet," I admit.

I begin scrolling through my phone, first time in several hours. My most recent text came from my girl Audre who is starting her shift at the same workplace as my husband.

AUDRE

Hey. Hope you're good and warm cuz its cold AF

Just got to work...I'm already tired lol. Cops pulled Skittles over. Had him leaning on his car in this cold while they searched his car. Smfh...

ME

Hey Dre. Crazy day here. Why would Skittles get pulled over? Did he get the officer's badge #?

I sigh after sending a reply to Audre, already knowing the answer to Harpreet's question.

"Let's say O'Malley was an old Black man and he spat in the face of a white detective," I say. "What would be the most likely outcome?"

"He would already be dead or fighting for his life right now from severe wounds," replies Harpreet.

"Exactly. I have two six-year olds who expect to see their mama tonight, so I best stay the hell away from that-"

"I got you. You may want to give your husband a heads up what happened. I saw at least three people catch it on video."

Oh great, the last thing I want is to answer questions to the media because of a video streaming on YouTube. March break couldn't come soon enough. That's the month I take some much-needed vacation time.

4

SIMEON

My second chance at employment was finally here and I'm amped. The assembly line isn't something that most workers look forward to but I'm a different cat. My actual career goal is to work at Sutton Motors. Perhaps it's low expectations, but it's all about having consistent money in my bank account.

I grew up in a Sutton Motors family. My parents are both Sutton retirees. All our vehicles in the driveway are Sutton-made. My brother Simon has been a Sutton employee for almost twenty years. And my family has always been pro-union. I'm so surrounded by the auto industry culture that I decided to embrace it- work at Sutton, buy a Sutton-made car, buy a house and retire in thirty years.

The turnover rate at Sutton is always low because of the union and the job security. As a result, the company went several years without hiring full-time workers. The year that my brother was hired, I was only thirteen. Four years later, Sutton was hiring again but I was still too young. Minimum requirements to be hired was eighteen and a high school diploma.

Optimistic that I would eventually work full-time for Sutton, I got hired as a Temporary Part-Time (TPT) worker, something that only current full-time post-secondary students could obtain. It went well, but once my two-year program was up, so was my job. And that was during a ten-year span when Sutton wasn't hiring any assembly workers.

Hiring continued unexpectedly four years ago. Sutton was accepting applications during a brief two-day period. Relatives of employees and former TPTs got first priority. Where the hell was I when the news broke? On a freaking seven-day Caribbean cruise with limited access to phone and Internet. Simon sent me numerous emails and text messages, but I was too busy getting drunk, high and eating all week. By the time I saw my brother's email, the deadline had passed. Afterwards, I went through three years of working various jobs and periods of depression until the opportunity came back in 2019. Mid-January 2020, I'm waiting for Simon to pick me up for my first day of my Sutton life.

"Whaddup Bruh," I say to Simon after I enter his SUV. "Ma said to come in the house after work. She's making lasagna for y'all."

"Nice, we haven't been able to cook the last few days with our kitchen being renovated," he answers. "Guy, what did I tell you about lighting up in my car?"

"Sorry, I'll roll down the window."

"No man, it's freezing. The moment I smell tobacco, it makes me wanna have a drink, and the last thing I wanna do right now is make a run to the liquor store and be late for work."

"You used to drink during work?"

"Two beers before shift, one during lunch. Did it for three years straight."

"And you never got caught?"

"Nope, only by the grace of God. I knew my job too damn well to get away with it. But I'm done drinking now. Haven't had one since Christmas Day."

"Wow. Okay then, I'll wait to smoke at work. But hey, can we quickly stop at a corner store? I need a pack."

Simon sighs. "Fine whatever."

I don't want to buy cigarettes from 7-Eleven, but my carton of cheap smokes from the First Nations reservation ran out and my friend isn't getting any until the weekend.

"So, how's life without alcohol?" I ask.

"Rough," Simon answers. "Worst month ever, but if it wasn't for God and attending church, I'd be-"

"You go to church now?"

Simon shakes his head. "Been going for a few months now, Sim. I told you this already. I swear you have the memory of a sausage sometimes."

"Sorry bro. A.D.D."

"No excuse, you ain't got A.D.D, not with a bartender diploma and the knowledge of mixing a hundred drinks."

"Mixologist. Not bartender, Mixologist."

"Sure. Anyways, this church is great bro. Faith Worship Tabernacle. You should come one of these Sundays."

"Nah I'm good. If I need church, I'll watch it online. Besides, if we work six days a week, when do I get a chance to sleep in?"

"How about everyday you're on afternoon shift? What time did you get up today, 1:30?"

"Noon, jackass. I'm more disciplined now."

He laughs. "Noon? That's impressive. So proud of you bro."

I give him the middle finger.

"Suck it up Sim, I'm just messing with you."

Smiling, I say, "Simon, this feels good. I'm finally a full-timer at Sutton. I feel like I've waited my whole life for this."

"That's weird to hear. Nobody, or should I say a very small few actually looks forward to a Sutton job."

"It's all I wanted to do. I blame you and our folks for this 'Sutton or Nuttin' concept. My goals are simple bro. After my 90-day probation is up, I'm finally buying my first brand new Sutton car. Then I'm gonna save cash for two years and buy a Condo. After that I'm good."

"That's it? No other goals for the next 28 years before retirement?"

"I just wanna build Sutton cars bro."

"Then Sutton is lucky to have you."

"Damn right!"

We both walk into the 7-Eleven and as usual, people gave us double takes. It was like they were thinking *Are they related?* but confused by our different shades of melanin. Simon and I have the same father but different mother. My mother is Black, but Simon's was a White woman. His mother died when he was only two. Dad re-married and they had me five years after.

"Two packs of Newport please," I say to the cashier while passing him my ID.

The cashier says, "You look like a skinny Black version of your friend."

I laugh, "That's because he's my brother. I'm better looking though. Add these mints please."

While I pay for my items, I notice a fine-looking lady enter the store that looks quite familiar. She walks past me without recognizing me at all, as if she's in a daze.

"Nezzie?" I call out to her.

She turns around and says, "Oh my God. I didn't notice you."

"How are you girl?" I hugged her but it's slightly awkward because she doesn't expect it. "Long time no see. You good?"

"Yeah, just trying to get my life back together, working and trying to stay outta trouble ha-ha. What about you?"

"Same here. I'm on my way to work now. Finally I'm working full-time at Sutton, today's my first day."

"Great. I'm working as a cashier at a supermarket. I'm just waiting for the bus to go home."

Inez "Nezzie" Martin, dated me a couple of years ago during my depressed state. Nezzie was going through some personal issues as well, so we were miserable together. All we did was have sex, drink, and get high on weed and occasionally coke when either of us had extra money. It wasn't a perfect relationship, but suddenly Nezzie stopped calling and texting me. Apparently, she found Jesus and changed her phone number. I was angry for a few days and then I moved on to other fish in the sea. But Nezzie was the first and only Black girl I ever slept with and seeing her reminded me of the good times we had together.

"Alright alright," I say. "I'm rushing out right now but it was good to see you. We should catch up some more, so can I call you?"

"Uh yeah, sure. Okay." Nezzie says with hesitancy. "Uh, give me your number and I'll call you so you can have mine."

I share my ten digits to her and she calls me as promised. Meanwhile, Simon pays for something and goes back to his truck.

"Cool. Take care Nezzie. We'll talk soon."

"Who dat?" Simon asks after I get in the truck.

"Girl I dated not too long ago. She put on some pounds but she's more good-looking now. She seemed kinda off though."

"How so?"

"Nezzie was high-energy when we dated. Her mind had no filter. In the store, she seemed super chill, almost boring."

"Maybe she's on meds."

"Think so? I thought it was because she aint doing drugs no more. That and religion, I mean apparently she left me after she started going to church."

Simon grins. "I like her already. Smart woman."

I gave him the finger again. "Love you too bro."

<u>5</u>

<u>SIMON</u>

Taking Simeon to work every day is something have to get use to until he's ready to buy his own car. Like many siblings, we clash quite a bit, but he's my only brother and I'm happy that he finally became a Sutton employee.

We went our separate ways in the plant and I decide to scroll through my phone while setting up my forklift vehicle. I'm a material handling driver that provides parts for assembly workers, so once the line starts, I don't have much time to check my messages.

AUDREE
Hey, check your boy Skid when you got some time. He got pulled over on the way here.
ME
Why, speeding?
AUDREE
Doubt it.
ME
Ok

I check to see if Skittles left me any text. Nope.

ME

Hey Skid, lemme know where you're working. I'll check you at lunch.

"Simon."

I look up from my phone and see my friend and new collegue Jessica Wallace. "Hey, how are you?" I smile. "Ready for another week in this joint?"

Jessica lets out a huge sigh. "Hope so. My first few weeks were rough Simon. I feel every muscle on my body right now, even muscles that I didn't know existed. I keep asking my husband how he managed to work here for almost twenty years, cuz I'm ready to quit now."

I grinn, "It gets better Jessica, trust me. We all went through the same pain. Unfortunately, some pain doesn't go away. That's why I drive a forklift now instead of doing assembly. Easier on my body."

"I don't blame you. So, if you and Darian been here almost twenty years, how old were you when you started at Sutton?"

"I was only twenty."

"Twenty? I'm forty-two. Huge difference. Ain't no way I'm working here for thirty years."

"I hear you. You shouldn't have to. Keep working on that Plan B. Keep working that Mary Kay stuff because the auto industry is unstable."

"Exactly. Speaking of Mary Kay, I had your wife's makeup that she bought from me at church yesterday but I didn't see her. Can I bring it to you tomorrow for you to give her?"

"Yeah of course. Speaking of, she's calling me now. I'll let her know."

"OK, tell her I said hi," Jessica waves as she walks away.

Normally my wife would text me before my shift instead of calling, so this might be important. "Hey luv."

"Hey. I left work early today," my wife says, sounding frustrated.

"You did? Why, are you ok?"

"No. Yes and no. We arrested Bill O'Malley, and in the process he spat in my face and called me a nigger."

The rage that instantly rose in my body wanted to unleash. But I had to respond with ease amid my shock. "Wha...are you serious? What the...how did you respond?"

"I didn't have to. Harpreet sucker punched him while I was in shock from the spit on my face. Now it's on video. Might be already on YouTube."

I sigh, although I'm ready to cry in anger.

"You have a damn good partner. I'm so sorry you had to endure that. What the hell man! Are you okay? I'm gonna come home and -"

"No Simon, it's fine."

"Tracey, are you sure? I'll leave right now so-"

"Simon, I'll be fine until you get home. I'm just going to order some food, cuddle and play with the kids, and have a glass of...damn."

"Have some wine tonight Tracey."

"No. We committed to stop drinking in 2020 and we've done well so far."

"Yeah, but Tracey how many people go through the amount of crap you deal with every day?"

My voice is louder than it needs to be. Some workers are staring at me but I don't care.

"I'm so mad right now Trace," I said as a hot tear falls down my cheek. "If I was there I would've beat the hell outta that old man and not think twice about it. And this scumbag distributes child porn?"

"Simon, keep your voice down! This is why I don't share everything that goes on at my job."

"Sorry hun. How do you deal with all this everyday? I couldn't, I mean...damn."

"Babe, it's only the grace of God. Not everyone can be a cop and not everyone can work in an assembly plant. But to deal with sex crimes, special victims and racism on a regular basis is tough. I could've easily put him in a hospital today, but thank God I'm going home to see my babies and you later. Haha, you're like the only White person I like right now."

I grin. "You don't like our Pastors?"

27

"Correction. Three White people. And your dad, so four. That's it. Love you babe, see you later."

"Bye. Love you too."

I'm doing my routes in the plant, removing empty large crates and returning full crates of vehicle parts. I say hello to the usual workers, union reps, and supervisors, but I'm angry. Angry and desperate for a drink. What would possess a man to release his nasty saliva on the face of a woman? Not just any woman, but a Black woman. Not just any Black woman, but my wife.

Tracey and I met at a summer backyard BBQ hosted by my childhood friend Audre and her late husband Hank. There was something about her entire persona that made me instantly attracted to her. She spoke with confidence, she was physically fit, and her dark chocolate skin. My stepmom played a major role into why I love confident Black women so much, so I wanted to know more about Tracey Rosen.

While we dated, I wasn't sure if I should get heavily involved with a woman who has a dangerous occupation. At times I would have sleepless nights, worried that she would be killed on the job. But the more Tracey shared about her love for the hurt and sought justice for them, the more I fell in love with her.

We got married and had children into our early thirties. Our six-year-old twins, Symon and Symone, were the perfect scenario for us, a boy and a girl in only one pregnancy term. However, our marriage has been far from perfect. Because Tracey is a detective, she's always on call. I work a day and afternoon shift rotation every two weeks. I constantly worry that one day I may become a single father. This anxiety, plus the regular stresses of life, led me towards alcoholism. However, it ended shortly after Jessica's husband Darian invited us to church several months ago.

Tracey and I became Christians after attending Faith Worship Tabernacle. We are still new to the faith but we are determined to live a godly life. Our biggest struggle is trying not to cuss and drink alcohol.

Our marriage is also getting better since we both agreed to this commitment.

I'm tempted to stop driving the forklift and browse YouTube to see if the video of the arrest is posted. However, I keep doing my job because if I watch the video, I will probably become more furious. I already want to severely hurt William O'Malley. Harpreet stepped in to defend my wife and, on my break, I'm going to text him a thank you.

There are many cases that Tracey refuses to give me details about because she works in the Special Victims Unit. I don't know how many rapists and perverts she's encountered, how many stories of victims she had to study, or how many derogatory words were directed to her on the regular. I refuse to ask unless Tracey is willing to discuss these matters. It's fine because I don't need to be an emotional mess every day.

My supervisor, Johnny, approaches me about a half hour into the shift. "Simon, we have extra drivers tonight. Do you wanna go home?"

That means I can leave but I won't be paid. Great news for me and I hear the choir in my mind singing Hallelujah! "Yeah sure, I'll go. Great timing."

"Good," Johnny says as he walks away.

Then, I receive a reply from Skittles.

SKITTLES

I'm working on the engine line. I gotta tell you what happened on my way here.

Shoot! I must tell him that I'll call him later because I'm going home. I was also going to visit Audre at lunch to see how her first day is going. But they will understand if I have to leave. My frustration came back when I think of Simeon, which made me shout an expletive.

"Johnny I gotta stay," I say to my boss as I approach his desk. "I forgot about my brother. He just started today and he doesn't have a ride home if I leave now."

"Shoot," he says with disappointment. "Ok, tell your team leader to send your replacement back to me."

I sigh as I go back to my vehicle. It's going to be a long shift.

<u>6</u>

<u>JESSICA</u>

Remember why you're doing this. God's got me. Keep pushing.

That's what I keep saying to myself as I work from car to car. It's tedious, it's boring and yes, it's painful. Every part of the right side of my body is hurting- the shoulder, arm, leg and foot. Not just sore, but they feel like fire. I keep doing the usual, open the driver door, inspect the seat, close driver door, open left rear door, inspect seat, close rear door, move to the next car, repeat. Four hundred cars or more every day.

I was told by my husband before working at Sutton that I will be a "floater", someone who does a different job on the line several times a week. After a month, I'm still waiting for this opportunity, because various jobs mean that I will use other ignored body parts. I've been on the same job since day one.

The advantage of being on the same job every shift is that I'm great at it. If I was working poorly the supervisor would've already placed me on another job, and Sutton is a workplace that has no problem telling someone they aren't performing well.

The con of doing a single job is that the active body parts start to weaken. The problem for me, is starting an autoworker career at forty-two years old, when many others begin in their early twenties. Another big problem is that I got hit by a truck six weeks before Sutton hired me. I was jogging in the evening just a block away from my home and the driver made a left turn without noticing that I was crossing the street. It was a miracle that I survived without any broken bones or a concussion. Every day, I thank the Lord that I'm able to be a good wife and mother to my husband and four kids, but my body is no longer the same. The truck injured the right side of my body, all the more reason why this job is excruciating.

While I'm pushing through work, with my earbuds connected, listening to a podcast, my supervisor Bobby Golic walks past me. He's a short man with blond spiked hair who comes across as arrogant, yet friendly. At least I thought so on my first day. He barely gives me a head nod. It's obvious to me that I'm no longer on his good side because of his current presumptions of me.

On my second day of assembly work, my body was having a difficult time adjusting to the tedious and monotonous pace. I seriously thought something was wrong, so I went to Bobby and asked to go to the medical office. The *you gotta be kidding* me expression he gave me afterward told me that Bobby labelled me as a slacker without knowing my medical history. So, I went to the office and told the nurse about my current condition. As I'm sitting in the waiting room, Bobby called the nurse to make sure I was there. After the nurse informed him of what I shared with her, I heard him say, "Well, I don't believe her" through the speakerphone.

That comment made me very upset. I don't know how many workers in Bobby's past had screwed him over with false medical claims just to escape working, but that wasn't fair of him to say that about me, especially on just my second day of work. My husband told me that the moment some new hires are done their 90-day probation, they apply for a medical leave. As a result, Bobby now has his guard way up about me and I've been nothing but a hard worker.

When I told my husband about Bobby's behavior that day, he was shocked and disappointed. Bobby used to be his supervisor and they had a good working relationship. But I'm a Black woman in a dominate-male workplace. Women already have the challenge trying to prove themselves in a "man's" work environment. Minority women must go the extra mile to fit in, with honest effort and a strong work ethic.

The more cars I work on, the more I want to just drop my equipment, grab my bag and leave Sutton, never to return. It's easier on my body to just home-school my four kids and focus on my Mary Kay business. I won't have to deal with the various personalities of management and workers. But it's the grace of God that keeps me pushing, in addition to the short and long-term goals my husband and I put together. Getting rid of our debt. Sending our kids to a private Christian school. Buying our first house. These goals are the only motives I need to get through another shift.

7

DARIAN

I have been called off my job to have a meeting with the supervisor and one of the men from upper management. It's my belief that I'm about to get written up for not wearing the Proper Protective Equipment (PPE) at my workstation.

My job is located at Underbody Chassis, which requires me to work underneath the Sutton vehicles, so it's mandatory that a safety hard hat must be worn. I hate how the padding feels inside the hat, so I took it out. But that's not how I got caught. Larry, an absentee specialist, was working across from me, covering for another worker for a short period of time. He was wearing a white baseball cap, making it obvious that he wasn't wearing a safety hat. While we were doing our tasks under the vehicle, the health and safety manager drives by in a golf cart. Sergei sees the shiny white cap and stops immediately.

When Larry was asked to wear a hard hat, he immediately starts to argue with Sergei. During the argument, Sergei noticed that my hard hat looked unusual.

"Are you wearing a hard hat?" he asks me. This man is asking me questions and I have no idea who he is.

"Yes I am," I answer but it isn't the full truth.

"Can you take it off please?"

I obey without hesitation and the truth is exposed. Sergei sees that the padding is removed and immediately reports the news to my boss. In the meantime, Larry manages to get off the assembly line and defends his guilty cause. I'm not fortunate enough to have that opportunity.

So now I'm accompanied with Ekene who's my Union representative as we sit across Sergei and Satnam, my supervisor.

"Darian, you know why you're here." Satnam says. "I'm very disappointed that you didn't take the time to wear your PPE."

He doesn't look disappointed. My boss just wants to sound politically correct next to Management. I don't respond until Satnam brings out the discipline papers for me to sign.

"So, can you answer me this?" I ask. "Is Larry getting written up as well? After all, Sergei wouldn't have stopped if he didn't notice Larry's violation first."

"Yes, I realize that," Sergei replies vaguely. To my defense, I should argue the matter further. Ekene points out that if I'm to be written up, Larry needs the same discipline to make it fair. However, I'm not a fan of conflict, so I sign the forms, accepting my punishment.

Ekene immediately puts in a grievance for my write-up but I don't think twice about it. Grievances usually take a year before it's handled and by then the discipline is off my employment record. What took place feels like an act of Systemic Racism. Sergei is White and so is Larry. I'm Black and the only one getting disciplined. Interesting.

With almost twenty years of seniority at Sutton, I have much bigger things to be concerned about, like making sure I help my wife keep our house in order after my shift is finished. The new routine is simple yet challenging- I take the van to work for the morning shift. However, if Jessica needs the van, she has to drop me for six in the morning. But today I have the van, so as soon as 2:30pm arrives, I'm dashing for the gates because I must pick up Jessica and drop her back at the plant for her 3:30pm shift. Then I have to make sure the kids are fed and the house is clean before going back to pick up Jessica at 11:30pm. By the time I fall asleep, it's usually 12:30am, only to wake up at 5am to repeat the routine. So, to put it lightly, I don't give a crap about getting written up for a safety hat.

It would be a different story if this happened to Jessica. She's on a probation and any discipline can lead to a dismissal. My former boss, Bobby, already let me down by the way he's judging Jessica as a lazy worker, which is so far from the truth. Because she and I work opposite shifts, I can't keep an eye on how supervisors are treating her. In my opinion, some White men are intimidated by strong Black women. All I can do is pray for God's protection over Jessica for every shift.

It's 7:30pm and I'm in my house cleaning the kitchen while the kids eat a late dinner. My four children, three girls and one boy ranging from age two to eleven, are an energetic bunch. Even while watching TV, they are busy with toys, crafts, and leaving a mess. They are currently being homeschooled until we can afford to send them to private school in the fall. Yes, my wife and I have our hands full.

A text from Jessica appears on my phone.

JESSICA
Can you pick me up please?
ME
Already? The shift is done?
JESSICA
Not yet
ME
Ok. Coming now

"This is a surprise," I say after Jessica steps inside our Dodge Caravan. "A good surprise cuz we can go to bed early."

"Yep," Jessica says. "The pain while working was getting unbearable, and I have a headache. So, I asked the supervisor if I could go home."

"Bobby didn't give you any issues?"

"No, Bobby's not my supervisor anymore. My new supervisor is some young guy named Chad. Do you know a Chad?"

"Hmmm, Chad. Tall White boy, always smiling? Looks like he graduated from high school yesterday?"

She laughs. "I know right? He's a nice guy. A little too touchy though, always placing his hand on everybody's shoulder."

"At least you don't have to deal with Bobby as much now."

"No," Jessica sighs. "So glad to be heading home. I can't wait to end my 90-day probation so I can book days off. My body needs the rest."

"I'm proud of you. You're pushing through, and I believe work will get better," I reply happily.

"In Jesus name. We know what we're trying to do- get rid of debt, buy a house, and keep our kids in Christian school. We just gotta stay focused, even though Lord knows I can't stand that place."

8

AUDRE

The shift is finally over and it feels like I just did a three-hour workout at the gym. The constant moving of the assembly line and trying to keep up with completing every job on every car is physically exhausting. The short breaks and lunch period is not enough recovery time. Thankfully, I have a great team leader on the door line that assists me for the majority of the shift. This is a culture shock for me, but my name is Audre Wilson and I don't let any obstacle overtake me.

"Do you still wanna work here?" my team leader, Gus, asks with a grin.

I answer, "Haha I'm not sure. My whole body is sore. I don't even feel like walking to my car."

"It'll get better. You did well today. By tomorrow, you'll be doing that job on your own."

"Cool. Thanks for your help. Good night."

Walking down the aisle feels like I'm a Go-Kart and everyone else a Lamborghini. I'm just excited to exit the gates, but every step hurts and I'm very tired. It's quite easy for Skittles to catch up to me.

"Dre you look like a penguin when you walk," he laughs.

"And you're walking normal," I reply. "Did you not work today?"

"Of course I worked. Remember, car parts are my life. They put me on the toughest job on the engine line and I was on my own after five minutes. I shocked everybody, including my clueless supervisor who said being a mechanic won't be an advantage for me. Dumbass."

"Only five minutes? I'm still not on my own after an entire shift, damn."

"That's normal though. You got this Dre," he grins while he pats my shoulder. I've never told Skittles, but when he smiles, he looks incredibly handsome. But I'm not ready to blow up his ego.

"Thanks bro," I say. "Hope your night made up for your episode with that officer. By the way, Tracey wants to know if you got his badge number."

"No," Skittles says. "Was I supposed to?"

I slap his arm. "Yes Skittles! You get his four-digit number, you can find out who he is! That pig doesn't have to tell his name."

"Damn. How did I not know that?"

"Well, now you know sweetie. Where's Simon and Simeon? Are they meeting us at the exit gate?"

"No. Simon told me he had to quickly drop Sim off and deal with an urgent matter at home."

I'm in shock. Tracey never messaged me about anything urgent. I messaged Simon during lunch, but he never responded back. "Oh. Did he give you any details?"

Skittles answers, "No, he said we will find out soon enough."

Driving home, I feel too fatigued that to put on the Bluetooth to listen to some Megan Thee Stallion. So, I keep it on the annoying news radio station. The same news every twenty minutes and it doesn't matter what time of day you listen; the news anchors sound the same. However, it's now 12:01am and I hear some very unexpecting news:

"*We start the hour with breaking news coming out of Georgetown. Halton Police have arrested multi-millionaire investor*

William O'Malley for his connections with distributing child pornography. O'Malley was arrested around 2:57 pm on Monday afternoon after apparently having an intense exchange with an employee. But the bigger story is video footage of O'Malley spitting in the face of Detective Tracey Harrison after being placed in handcuffs..."

"WHAT THE FA--" I yell. I gotta hear the rest of the story.

"...calling her a derogatory name. Harrison's partner Harpreet Singh responds by punching O'Malley in the face and escorting him out of the diner. We will have more information on this story as it develops on 580 News."

"WHAT! SOME OLD ASS WHITE MAN LET OUT SOME NASTY SPIT IN MY GIRLS' FACE? HELLL NO, HELL NO! GOOGLE, CALL SKITTLES!" I shout in anger.

The phone keeps ringing through the speaker. Voicemail. I press the end button and try again.

"Boy, why ain't you picking up your phone? You know who's calling-"

I suddenly remember that Skittles was pulled over for touching his phone. He's playing it safe driving home. So, I hang up. My boy doesn't need another Driving While Black event.

Suddenly, I'm wide awake and I drive home as fast as I can to watch the video.

After I park, I wait for the Wi-Fi signal from the house to activate on my phone and I watch the video clip in my van. I'm shocked, horrified, anxious and angry all at the same time. Tracey needs some encouragement from me but she's with Simon right now, which is more important.

Skittles calls me back. "Hey."

"Sorry I wasn't trying to answer my phone while driving, for obvious reasons," he says apologetically.

"I realized that after the fact, my bad Skid. Tracey was spat in the face by an old ass white man and it was caught on video! And he called her a nigger!"

"What? Where'd you see it?"

"Freaking TMC.com. How the hell did they get this video so fast?"

"When people know that the paparazzi pays, they'll send anything. Send me the link."

"Doing it now. It hurts to know that Tracey deals with that bull-"

I stop because I notice that the backyard lights turn on. We have two entrances to our walkout basement apartment: the side door and the sliding door to the backyard. We always us the side door.

"Skittles, lemme call you back tomorrow, or just text me later."

I get out the van and walk to the backyard. There are footprints in the snow leading to the sliding door. Immediately, I think someone is trying to break in, but the light would send them away. Thankfully, it's my son Terrell hoping to sneak in the house before I reach home. He didn't fully close the blinds after closing the sliding door, so I see Terrell taking off his coat and talking to Tristan. He probably feels like he got away with being out way past his curfew. It's time for his rude awakening.

BANG! BANG! BANG!

The twins jump in fear like they are in a haunted house. I wanted to laugh my ass off, but I was too cold and pissed off. "Why you look so scared?" I ask Terrell after he opens the door. "Did you do something wrong?"

"Uh, how was work Mama?" he responds.

"Don't 'how was work Mama' me. Why did you come through these doors two minutes ago? And why do you smell like weed?"

"Um...I was at Ricky's house and fell asleep watching a movie. When I woke up it was 11:30pm."

"If you're tired, then you come home before your 10:00pm curfew! Do I need to call Ricky's mother to confirm you were at their house?"

"You can Mama, but she's at work."

I sigh and look at Tristan. "Why are you still in your school clothes? Why is the TV loud like we at the movie theatre? Turn it off!"

Tristan obeys quickly.

"Terrell Howard Wilson, let this be your final warning. Forget 10:00pm, 9:30pm is now your curfew. Why the hell do you need to be out on a cold night in January anyway? Stay your ass home. Like I told your brother, when I get home, I expect a clean and quiet apartment. My body is busted from this new job, so my tolerance for disobedience has gotten lower. If this happens again, you will lose your phone. Got it?"

"Yes Mama," Terrell says.

"Yes Mama," Tristan repeats.

"Now get out of my sight until 8:00am when y'all better be ready for me to drop you to school."

An hour later, after an Epson Salt bath, I'm ready for bed. I go to the kitchen for a light snack and see Terrell by the fridge.

"Just getting some water Mama," he says.

"Um hum," I reply. "Terrell, do you enjoy listening to White people call us nigger?"

"Of course not Mama."

"Then why didn't you follow your brother when he left class, while your teacher was saying it like it wasn't a big deal?"

To escape an immediate answer, Terrell takes a huge sip of water. "I had basketball after school."

"Poor excuse. I said 'left class'. You didn't have to leave school. Your Aunt Tracey was spat on and called a nigger by an old White man today. If you think everyone loves a cool good-looking Black guy that's good at basketball, you'll be in for a rude awakening."

9

SIMON

This may have been the longest shift in my twenty years of working at Sutton. I drop Simeon home and thankfully my parents are sleeping, so there won't be any unnecessary chit-chat. My wife needs me home with her. The video is getting viral and the last thing Tracey needs is to watch any news or social media. Hopefully, she's in a peaceful and relaxing mood.

I enter my house and it's mostly clean, except for the renovation clutter in the kitchen. The twins are fast asleep in the kids bedroom upstairs. My two bundles of joy. Symon and Symone are unaware of the crazy work environments of Tracey and me. They see Mommy, Daddy, their grandparents and they think that Black and White equals love. I wish we all could think that way.

As I walk into our master bedroom, the King size bed is still made up. Tracey isn't in our bathroom. I put on my pajamas, then proceed to the basement.

The music is loud, but not noisy enough to disturb the neighbors. It's one of our favorites, 90s East Coast hip-hop. Tracey is in her gym outfit kickboxing the hell out of the punching bag, showing no mercy.

"Tracey!" I yell as I get closer to her. No response so I get closer to the bag.

I repeat, "Tracey!" It's like I'm not in the room whatsoever. She's laser-focused on the punching bag, one jab after another, kick after kick. It looks like she wrote *O'MALLEY* at the top of the bag with a permanent black marker. I grab the stereo remote and press the stop button.

Tracey is startled, as if I woke her up from a bad dream. "Wha...hey. When did you get home?"

"Few minutes ago," I say. "You can stop now, O'Malley is pretty tore up."

"Damn. I was really zoned in..."

As she says that, Tracey falls backwards from exhaustion, but I'm able to catch her in time. "Ok babe, time to go upstairs," I say as I take off her boxing gloves and lead her up the stairs. "Your day is done."

After Tracey comes out of the shower, I turn off the TV in our bedroom. "I saw the video. God, if that was me instead of Harpreet-"

"I know babe," Tracey says. "I'm glad it wasn't you because you'd be in prison right now. I love you as my autoworker husband and not a Cop. That's not to say you aren't tough, as I've told you many times before."

I immediately regret the comment. My occasional insecurities about not being a tough guy rears its ugly head at the worst time. I have to shift the discussion. "How are you feeling?"

"Honestly I feel better. The punching bag received most of my anger and frustration. Once the kids fell asleep, I took out the bottle of wine and I poured a glass, but I couldn't drink any of it."

"Why not? After what you went through?"

"I remembered how well we've been doing without drinking and I didn't want to relapse. So, I turned off my phone and the media devices and just prayed. Shortly after, I started kickboxing."

"You're better than me. I would've drunk the whole damn bottle. You are so badass, and I can't love you enough."

She kisses me as we get into bed. "Thank you baby, love you too." Then she sighs. "It's gonna be a circus at the station tomorrow. The media's all over this story."

"Can you blame them? Especially with a well-known man like O'Malley. I'll be praying for you all day."

"I'll need it. Hey, how did Dre, Sim and Skittles do today? Dre told me Skittles got pulled over?"

Her voice is fading. Sometimes she chats herself to sleep.

"I think it went good," I answer, "but to be honest, I didn't ask. I'll talk more to Skittles about what happened tomorrow."

No response. Tracey is out cold.

Twenty minutes later, I'm in the kitchen grabbing the wine bottle from the fridge. Tracey's events stressed me out and this is a reason why she limits her conversations about work. As I'm about to take a sip, I yell out an expletive and dump the entire bottle down the drain. I honestly don't know how, but I'm going to overcome this struggle.

10

TRACEY

Driving to work, I turn on Hallelujah FM on the IHeart Radio app. I had my fight music old school fix the night before, but now I need the Peace of God to surround me. It's going to be an unusual day and I need the Lord to fight my battles.

The image of that dirty old man spitting in my face won't leave. I've encountered many disturbing events as a cop, but what he did was more than a crime. It was hate. And now, I will have to address the details to the public.

I park my car along the street and walk to the back of the police station. Unfortunately, a couple of reporters are waiting for me but I keep on walking.

"Detective Harrison, what was your immediate reaction when William O'Malley spat in your face?"

"Detective, how would you have responded if Detective Singh didn't punch O'Malley?"

"What are your-"

I close the door and proceed to my division unit. I greet the lovely receptionist as usual and go to my cubicle. Turn on my computer and unlock my file drawer, ready to focus on solving cases. Anything to get my mind off of yesterday.

Harpreet enters the room with Tim Hortons drinks in a tray. "G'mornin Tracey," he says. "Got your large Iced Capp with an Expresso shot."

"Thank you Preet. I almost texted you to grab me one. Good looking out partner."

"That's a lot of sugar in the morning though."

"Same as your two blueberry muffins, so don't judge me. How did the questioning go yesterday?"

"O'Malley was all over the place. Went from angry and unapologetic to crying and remorseful. Clearly he has a mental disorder and he may use it as his defense."

"No excuse for calling me a nigger. The hate in his heart came out in the wash. There's no doubt that O'Malley is guilty."

"Yep. Now it's about how much he'll get away with."

"Unfortunately."

"Your husband sent me a text thanking me for having your back."

"He did?" I ask with surprise. "Simon is grateful. It was hard for him to see the video. I still haven't seen it. Not trying to."

"I wasn't trying to either until I had people DMing me to check out the YouTube comments. Unbelievable."

"Really, were they mostly good or bad?"

"You be the judge," Harpreet said as he views his phone. "Like this- 'What that cop did was sexy AF...I've never been so attracted to an Indian in my life...How can I get arrested by this man, he needs to handcuff me to my bed.' Plus a bunch of GIFs and memes. I don't know. It's crazy for me to talk about this when such a hateful act happened to you."

It does sound crazy, but my partner is one of the most genuine cops I've ever worked with. Hearing that he's viewed as a celebrity and hero is something worth smiling about. "Your Tinder account's about to blow up."

"Damn," he shakes his head. "I'm not even gonna open it."

"Stop lying, you know you will," I laugh.

Our Detective Sergeant, Liam Anderson, walks towards us. He is one of a handful of officers that I've worked with since day one; almost sixteen years ago. Always a professional, almost to a fault. We've had numerous disagreements in the past, but I have a great deal of respect for his leadership.

"I'm glad to see you in here instead of dealing with the growing circus outside," Liam says. "Both of you did an excellent job yesterday. My advice would be to stay away from any news or social media until your shift is done."

"Got it," Harpreet says.

"Don't have to tell me twice sir," I say.

"Great," Liam says. "Harrison, can I see you in my office for a moment?"

"Uh yeah," I say as I follow him. Liam closes the door.

"Have a seat," he says. "First of all, I want your honest feelings. Are you okay?"

I sigh. "I'm okay to work, but I'm not okay. The thought of that man's stink saliva spreading on my face won't leave my mind. A big part of me wishes that Harpreet didn't step in. I wrote 'O'Malley' on my punching bag and went at it for an hour last night."

"Well, I'm glad Harpreet stepped in. I would have preferred he did, then the alternative, suspending you for killing an old man. The best justice is to have O'Malley locked up for as long as possible."

"I agree, but I can't stand hate. I can't stand perverts and O'Malley is both. He better pay."

"And you know Harrison, there is counseling available if what happened is affecting your job and family."

"Yes, I know." I hate the reminder, but it's something I must consider if my current mood doesn't get improve.

Liam says, "There's another reason why I want to talk to you. Bill Simpson is transferring to another department next month. As you know, he was a Sergeant Major here and now I've been promoted to that position."

"Sergeant Major?" I say. "That's great, congratulations! Well-deserved sir."

"Thank you. But now that leaves the Detective Sergeant position available. I'm going to put in a high recommendation that you get this position."

I'm nervous. The Detective Sergeant oversees directing the SVU, like Olivia Benson of Law & Order SVU. I picture myself eventually moving up the police ranks, but not this soon in my career. Not this soon in a department and region that's not too friendly to employees of color.

"Wow sir, I... that would be, wow I didn't see this coming."

"I don't know anyone here that would fill the position better than you," Liam adds. "You bring integrity to this department, you are resilient, fearless and you don't overstep the rules. And of course, you're a woman of color which makes the Halton Police look really good."

"I appreciate your recommendation and the kind words Sir, but may I ask you not to get my hopes up about this and then not get the position? Now that you told me, it's all I'm going to be thinking about."

"I wouldn't tell you this if your chances weren't very high. I just wanted to give you a heads up. The transitions are happening, but there hasn't been an official announcement yet. Think it over and discuss it with your husband. If you want it, this is the opportunity to get it and I will do my best to help make that happen."

As I leave his office, I think of how good the Lord is. Even during a storm, He has a diamond in the rough. The only person I'm going to notify of this opportunity is Simon, whenever the chaos of this day comes to an end.

11

SKITTLES

Today, I arrive at work at 2:40pm, fifty minutes before start time. I drove under the speed limit and didn't touch my phone whatsoever. To be safer I didn't even touch any buttons on the center console. I am determined never to be stopped by the cops again, although as a Black man this is very unlikely.

Before arriving to work I made a stop at Burrito Girlz for Taco Tuesday. I wasn't buying tacos, but burritos are good enough, same culture. I bought four of the Big Sexy, which are twelve-inch monsters. Two for myself and one each for the Harrison brothers. My goal is to have a stress-free day.

Simon and Simeon arrive at the lunch table I'm sitting at, enjoying my first Big Sexy. I give them both fist pumps as Simon sits across from me.

"Thanks brah," Simeon says as I give him his burrito. "I'll e-transfer you the cash. This has extra guacamole, right?"

"Yeah," I answer. "You good man? How was your first day on the Trim line?"

"Money. Didn't miss a beat bro. But hey, let's catch up later cuz I'm going for a smoke."

"Alright, for sure."

Simon says, "Hey Sim. Remember about the video."

"No worries bro, I got you," Simeon says as he walks away.

"I told Sim not to show anyone the video, and if anyone talks about it, not to let them know Trace is his sister-in-law."

"How's Tracey doing? It's one thing going through that trauma but then have it exposed to the world. I must've seen it at least ten times already."

"That's nine times more than me. Of course she's angry about it, more so of the fact that the footage is out there. But by God's grace, we'll get through this. Funny though, a lot of people here know that my wife's a cop, but they don't know where she works and what kind of cop she is. I don't know how long that will last though."

"Well, I won't mention it to anybody. I love y'all too much to add more stress to your life."

"Thanks bro. Yo, how much stuff did you put in your burrito? Half of it is dripping out."

I say, "Haha, it's the goodness bre-drin. It has steak, brown rice, double black beans, lettuce, tomatoes, onions, jalapeno, ghost pepper sauce, corn, pinto beans, chipotle BBQ sauce, sour cream, ranch, suicide hot sauce, guacamole, and salsa."

"Da hell? All those beans and pepper? What, you trying to kill a cop with farts if they pull you over?"

I laugh, even though I'm still pissed about my DWB interrogation. "Damn, I should've known about taking that cop's badge number. I can't even file a proper complaint."

"Want me to see if Tracey can get it for you?"

"Nah. I'll let it go. As long as it never happens again."

"I hear you. So how was working on the engine line yesterday?"

"It went smooth. Easier than-"

"Sorry Skid, Tracey's calling," Simon grabs his phone. "I'll come by later."

"Alright bro."

We pump fists and he walks away. I continue to enjoy my Big Sexy and suddenly a lovely looking lady named Donna decides to sit across from me, who I met while I was on the line yesterday. My team leader, Carl, had finished training me on my job and asked if I wanted a quick washroom break. I declined, and that's how we started talking as we worked across from each other.

"Word of advice, if someone offers you a break, take it," she advised. "Our official breaks are short. Doing that job now may be ok, but let's see how you feel after four hundred engines."

I smiled, "You obviously know this from experience."

"Twelve years. This your first day?"

"Yes."

"I'm Donna. Welcome to the Sutton Engine line."

"I'm Skittles. Nice to meet you."

"Skittles?" Donna laughed. "How fitting."

"How so?"

"During break, someone at the lunch table said you were eye candy."

I smiled, "I hope that was a woman who said it."

"Does it matter?" Donna winked with a grin and continued to work, ending the conversation.

In my opinion, she reminds me of a sports mom in her late thirties. Donna has short brunette hair, tanned Caucasian skin, tall, and smells lovely. I quickly wipe off my face and hands to look presentable.

"That looks good," Donna says about my burrito. "Wish I had stopped to pick up food before coming to work. Going to the cafeteria takes up half the lunch break and it's not worth the price."

"Yeah. This tastes so good," I answer. "Got it from Burrito Girlz."

"Ahh, the joint where all the workers show cleavage."

"Hmmm, I don't know what you're talking about," I lie with a grin.

"Yeah okay," she laughs. "You look like you're fitting in very well so far. That is the toughest job on the engine line, and you made it look easy."

"Thanks. It's probably because I'm quick with my hands or my exceptional mechanical expertise or maybe both. It's going better than I thought."

Donna's blue eyes lights up. "You're a mechanic? Great! Can I ask you a question about the tires on my car? Last weekend, I got winter tires installed and suddenly I'm hearing a grinding noise. Did they install it correctly?"

While she is speaking, I give my buttocks a hard squeeze. It's a huge fart and I'm praying it doesn't smell. "Does it grind while you drive or when you slow down?"

"When I slow down," Donna answers. "Wait, is it my brakes?"

"Probably. Whoever put on your tires failed to inform you that you need new brake pads, and maybe routers too."

"Damn. Last thing I need is to dish out more money."

"I can replace your brakes," I suggest while keeping my butt tight. "Lemme call my guy and see how much the parts will cost. What vehicle do you drive?"

"A 2015 Sutton Topaz. When can you do it? The brakes sound really bad."

"I can give you a quote tomorrow morning and I can install them by noon."

"Oh great, thank you!" Donna smiles as she gets up from the table. "I'll give you my number next break, cuz I'm gonna run to the washroom before we start running."

"No problem."

I grin as Donna leaves, thinking about the possibility of making extra money outside the plant. If word gets around that I'm a certified mechanic, tax-free cash will be a regular thing.

What isn't regular is the latest passing of gas. It feels like liquid. I look at my phone and the time is 3:27pm. Only three minutes until the buzzer. Horrible timing.

I don't want to, but I sprint-walk down the aisle and run upstairs to the washroom. This is going to be the quickest number two ever. I have no choice because its 3:28pm.

Open the first stall. No toilet paper.

I open the second stall. Clogged toilet.

The third stall has urine all over the seat.

The fourth and final has a toilet in good standing. Usually, I place toilet paper over the seat as a cover, but I have no time. I drop my pants, sit down, and it squirts out like a person laughing while their mouth is filled with chocolate milk. It seems like it's complete, so I grab a huge wad of toilet paper, wipe and flush. Less than a minute before the buzzer. While I bend over to do an unsatisfactory hand wash over the sink, the feeling down below comes back stronger.

"OH, HELL NO!" I yell as I run back to the stall.

The buzzer goes off at the same time my ass erupts. I feel a panic attack approaching. At the work orientation last week, the discussion leader stated that when the assembly line moves, I must be at my job. If I'm not on my job, the part isn't assembled and the line needs to stop. The longer the stop, the lower the daily vehicle build, which affects Sutton's bottom line.

I'm more worried about Sutton Motors than my current condition. It's only my second day and I'm scared of getting suspended or fired. I wish Donna gave me her number because I have no contacts for anyone on the engine line.

One eruption comes after another. I'm sweating and my nose is running. This is a punishment for my gluttony and I'm praying to the Lord for wisdom out of this situation. I can't leave until my deposit is complete. Although the longer I stay, the more trouble I'm going to receive from management. I think about Simon and grab my phone.

ME

Simon, can you please let my supervisor know that I'm in the washroom and I'm not feeling well?

I press SEND but seconds later it reads "Failed to send message." No reception in the washroom.

Another eruption happens. All I can do is close my eyes and wait until I'm not full of it anymore.

I feel dirty, yet so much better. I run back to the engine line ten minutes later. The line is moving but everyone is staring at me. My team leader is doing my job.

"You're still here!" Carl shouts. "We thought you quit and went home. Where were you? The line was down for seven minutes."

"Emergency. Washroom," I admit as I put on my gloves and notice four men in business casual attire at Brad's desk. "Who are those guys?"

"Uh, the Chassis Manager, Assistant Chassis Manager, our Union rep and the Assistant Plant Manager. If the line is down for more than five minutes, management comes like flies to feces."

"Oh. I got the next engine, thanks Carl. Am I in trouble?"

"Hope not. Any questions, just talk to our Union Rep."

I begin working as if everything is normal. Donna who works several feet across from me asks me if I'm okay, looking very concerned. I nod and look away. Most of the time I'm an open book but I'm not going to tell a woman that I almost crapped my pants.

Brad approaches me with his arms folded. "Do you know what time the line starts?"

I say, "Yes, 3:30pm."

"Then, where the hell were you? Running on CPT?"

Did this shrimp just say the acronym for Colored People Time? I'm so ready to fire back but I'll stay civil.

"In the washroom," I answer. "Last minute emergency, it was really bad."

"Then why didn't you let me know before you went?"

Say what?

I shout, "Because if I came to your desk before going to the washroom, I would've crapped my pants and you wouldn't have seen me for the rest of the day!"

Now I'm embarrassed and pissed. I feel as if Brad wants me to lose my cool to give him more of a reason to fire me.

"Just watch yourself," Brad says. "This isn't the garage like you're used to. We have rules here."

"What the hell Brad, leave him alone!" Carl shouts. "It's only his second day, calm your ass down!"

Thank God my team leader stepped in because I'm ready to rip Brad a new one.

He responds, "Well, you tell him the rules and regulations of working here!"

Brad walks away. Other guys on the line start dissing him out loud, talking about his ineptness as a supervisor.

"Man, is he like this every day?" I ask.

"Brad's an arrogant prick who has no filter," Carl said. "That's why we don't have a problem getting lippy with him. Most of the time he deserves it."

"I have no problem putting Brad in his place, but I just wanna get through my probation first."

12

SIMON

"Hey luv, how's your day going?"

"Hey babe," Tracey says. "It's been crazy, but not so much with the media yet. Just staying busy. Taking a quick lunch break at my desk right now. How are my babies?"

"They're fine, even though Symone fussed the entire drive to school. After we got there, she was fine. Symon was too tired to eat his breakfast."

"They were up later than usual, 10:30pm. Tonight they have to be in bed no later than 7:30pm."

"Okay. Your phone must be flooded with texts because mine has been buzzing non-stop."

Tracey sighs. "It's been ridiculous! It's even buzzing right now. Anyways, I didn't call you about the video. Liam is being promoted to Sergeant Major, so the Detective Sergeant position is going to be open and he says there's a very strong chance that I'll get it."

"Detective Sergeant? Wow, that's great news! No one deserves this more than you."

"Thanks, but it's not confirmed. There's a chance it may not happen and that's why I'm only telling you."

"OK. But if it happens we're celebrating. Nothing big, but it'll be special."

"Well babe, let's wait for the official news before making plans, ok?"

"Of course. I'm praying for you out there, love. Stay away from any social media and the texts until you at least get home, and even then keep it to a minimal. I gotta go love, but text me anytime. I'll call you on my lunch. Love you."

"Love you too, bye."

I end the call with mixed feelings about Tracey's news. We pray daily for success with our jobs and finances, so a promotion to Detective Sergeant will be great for my wife. Tracey is very smart and tough as nails, so she will be great as a leader of the SVU. But I could barely sleep last night after what happened to her yesterday. Will a promotion increase or decrease the targets on Tracey's back? As my worries for her elevate, I realize that I have the bigger issues. I knew what I was getting myself into when I married a Black female police officer. It's a must for me to be supportive and trust that God will protect her from harm every single day.

The shift begins but the Final assembly line runs for only ten minutes, stopping for an unknown reason. As a driver in Material Handling, I continue to do my job regardless of if the line is moving or not. But after ten minutes of stoppage, some workers decide to sit down and wait, so I decide to take a short break as well. I go to a nearby table where two guys are chatting- Gus, who I've known for over ten years and a new employee named Travis, a carefree kid who's all about working to have fun.

"Gus, the guys you recommended for house renovations are doing a great job with my kitchen. Thanks again."

"That's good brother," Gus answers. "Those dudes do great work."

"What's going on? Why is the line down?"

"I have no idea. Something happened on the engine line because they were down for the first seven minutes apparently."

"Oh ok." I take out my phone and begin to scroll through my texts. My parents, Skittles, Darian, and numerous others are waiting for my reply. The most notable message was from my pastor Marvin Bailey, who wants me to call him whenever I have an opportunity. He must have seen the video.

"Gus, check this out man," Travis says, passing him his phone. "Did you hear about this yesterday?"

Since I'm sitting next to Gus, I glance at Travis' phone. It's the video! I don't know how to respond. I feel warm, but I'm glad they have no idea the detective is my wife.

"That's William O'Malley?" Gus asks. "What the hell! He spat in that Black cop's face!"

"Yeah bro, you see that punch though?" Travis asks.

"Oh damn! Simon, you seen this?"

I nod, biting my tongue in disgust.

"That's abuse bro," Travis says. "Straight up abuse!"

Gus says, "Yeah well, at least the cop let him know he can't get away with spitting on a female cop, a Black female cop."

"Naw man, it's abuse what the cops did to O'Malley!"

My eyes grow wide in shock. Did I hear Travis correctly?

"Say what?" Gus asks. "What abuse? O'Malley was handcuffed, and he called the officer a nigger after he spat on her! That man deserves more than a punch in the face for that and being a child porn distributor!"

"That's wrong. O'Malley wouldn't do nothing like that. O'Malley is a legend in the Georgetown community. He has given so much to the people there- from employment to charity events. When I was a little kid, our family had nothing for Christmas because my mom only had a minimum wage job. Somebody told O'Malley about it and his organization gave me and my brother a big bag full of gifts, groceries for the house, and paid our rent for a whole year. No man would care that much for families and then get involved with child porn. That's a ridiculous charge, he's being set up!"

"Travis, just because a man does good for a community doesn't make him a saint," Gus explains. "Look at Bill. He was making family shows and was all about education, but now he's in jail for date raping women."

"Well, I believe he's being framed! Spitting on that Black woman is gonna look like a hate crime, but that's what she gets for wrongfully arresting a highly respectable man!"

BANG!

That's my knee hitting the table. Anger rushes through my body and I'm ready to choke the life out of this ignorant young buck. Travis is obviously comfortable speaking his mind around a table where everyone is his skin color. I'm seeing red. How dare this little piece of crap think that my wife deserved what O'Malley did to her?

Gus says, "Damn, you okay Simon? What's your take on this ridiculous statement? Isn't your wife a cop?"

"Yeah, my wife is a cop," I say as I get up and walk towards Travis. "Did you know that Travis?"

"Uh, no." he says, puzzled as to why I'm approaching him.

"And Gus, you may not know this either because you're not on IG or Facebook, but not only is my wife a cop, but a Black cop."

Gus says, "I didn't know that brother."

"All good. So Travis, do you know the name of the black female officer in that video? Did you care to research that info?"

Travis mutters, "Uh uh."

"Lemme help you out. Detective Tracey Harrison."

"Ahhh damn!" Gus says as he lowers his head on the table. "Simon I didn't know man, I'm so sorry."

I'm not even looking at Gus. My eyes of fury stay focused on Travis, who's turning red and looks nauseated.

"Simon, my bad man I'm sorry," he cries. "I-"

"Shut the hell up! Shut. The. Hell. Up. You're not sorry. You're saying sorry cuz I'm ready to beat the mess outta you. You got that same racist spirit that's been plaquing Georgetown for years. The same hate spirit that gave my dad death threats to make him move out of Georgetown because he married a Black woman. You got a serious heart problem. My advice to you is to not say another word to me, otherwise I will get violent. And I don't give a damn if you report this to the Union because I'll just tell them you promote hate. You better watch your ass boy, or your next beatdown won't be from me."

As soon as I say that, the assembly line starts to move. I'm still giving him the death stare. Travis wants me to leave because he's obviously nervous and embarrassed from everyone staring at us. So I walk back to my cart and drive away.

Placing my Airpods in my ears, I play some music and try not to focus on what just occurred. But it's hard because the situation still bogs my mind as to how much hate is in this world, including my workplace. I really need a hard drink.

13

AUDRE

Four hours into the shift of my second day and it's going pretty well. My entire body is sore, but they have me on the same job as yesterday so it's making the shift go smoother. Lunch time arrives and I'm way more prepared for the meagre twenty minutes- a sandwich and salad instead of cooked food and waiting to use a microwave. I need any extra minute I can get.

The time flew by and it's mostly due to working next to a lady that really knows how to chat. Margaret has been at Sutton for twenty-five years who seems to know every worker. She also seems like someone to ask for valuable insight and juicy rumors, but not trustworthy enough to share my confidential info. But I'm glad to meet someone who makes me feel more comfortable at Sutton.

"So Audre, how did you get into Sutton?" Margaret asks.

"Uh, just like yesterday, I scanned my card and I was allowed through the gate," I grin.

"Oh God, I like you. Feisty one-liner jokes like my husband."

"Sorry I had to do it. I got into here through my friend Simon. He works in Material Handling."

"I know Simon. I can still remember his first week here twenty years ago. Boy was cocky, thought he was something special because his parents worked here. Complained to the Union about everything."

"Really? Simon Harrison? I mean, I've known him my whole life and he's always been opinionated but he's not arrogant now as a husband and father."

"That's because he got humbled. After a few weeks of acting entitled, word got out to his parents about his behavior. His stepmother came to Simon while he was working on the line and gave him a strong rebuke. Simon was so embarrassed, he became a nice man ever since."

I laugh, "Theresa Harrison don't play! You don't wanna get on her wrong side."

"Damn right! But if you're on Theresa's good side she's a-"

SLAM!

I jump to the sudden noise next to me. A big White man with a thick beard slams an Asian man onto the table next to us, choking his neck.

"I KNEW YOUR PUNK ASS WAS SCREWING MY WIFE!" the choker snaps.

"I... thought...you were separated," the victim says despite his difficulty to breathe.

"SEPARATED AIN'T THE SAME AS DIVORCED, YOU LIL' SH-!"

"HEY!" yells a petite white lady marching toward the choker. "FREDDY, LEAVE JAMIE THE HELL ALONE!"

"Back off Suzette!" Freddy warns her.

Suzette starts pounding his back with her fists which annoys Freddy more than hurts him. "I SAID BACK THE HELL OFFA HIM NOW!"

Because of her high pitch voice, a small crowd of workers and management are gathering. Freddy saw his supervisor and releases his grip off Jamie's neck. Jamie kneels on the ground, coughing dramatically.

"This ain't done!" Freddy said. "Don't let me see you around my wife-"

Suzette yells, "HOW BOUT YOU SHUT THE HELL UP! IF YOU WERE A BETTER HUSBAND THIS WOULDN'T BE HAPPENING RIGHT NOW!"

"IF YOU WOULD KEEP YOUR LEGS CLOSED FOR ONCE, YOU'D-"

"ALRIGHT, THAT'S ENOUGH!" a supervisor yells. "SAVE THIS FOR COUNSELING SESSION AND LET EVERYONE ENJOY THEIR LUNCH!"

"Why do I feel like I had front row tickets to Jerry Springer?" I ask Margaret after the crowd goes away.

Margaret answers, "It was a storm waiting to happen. Suzette and Freddy, the big dude, split up last year after Freddy slept with a co-worker on the other shift. A one-night stand apparently. Freddy's been begging for her forgiveness since then, but Suzette started messing with Jamie as revenge sex. That was several months ago. Revenge sex turned into an actual relationship, and Freddy just found out it was still going on."

"That's messed up. Is there anything you don't know about this place?"

"Yeah. I don't know how I'm gonna finish this food in four minutes when I gotta pee. This salad is too good for me to quit. I'll just get Gus to give me a relief once the line starts after lunch."

"That kid was assaulted and threatened. Is Freddy gonna get fired?"

"Nah. Sutton will try to, but the Union will fight for him. He'll probably get a few days suspension and that's it."

I finish my lunch, which is a Kale salad with no dressing, cashews and water. Why did I make such a dull meal? Maybe because in this plant and outside this workplace, life is anything but boring.

14

SIMEON

The buzzer goes off for lunch and I'm eagerly looking forward to eating my Big Sexy Burrito. But with only twenty minutes for lunch, being a smoker is challenging. I literally have to time my agenda: six minutes to eat, nine minutes to smoke, and five to take a piss and return to my workstation.

As I'm devouring my burrito, I feel a soft hand on my shoulder. It's my supervisor Juanita Velez.

"Just wanna say you're doing well and I'm really happy you're working in my area," she says with a pretty smile.

"Oh," I reply with my mouth full. "Thanks Juanita."

I can't help but notice her tight booty as she walks away.

"Man, I would so tap my supervisor if I had a chance," I tell my buddies Lance and Adam outside in the smoking zone. "Juanita is fine as hell."

Lance says, "She would never date a junkie like you. You can tell she takes care of her body. When's the last time you went to the gym?"

I suck my teeth as I take a puff. "Whatever. I didn't say I was gonna ask her out."

Adam says, "I wouldn't overestimate Juanita bro. I heard she has a wild side outside this plant. Just look, she's in her mid-forties with no wedding ring."

I ask, "What stories have you heard?"

"Hold on." Adam is staring at his phone with a big grin. "Yo, the guy that I was telling y'all about yesterday has some Blow to sell tonight after work in the West parking lot."

Lance says, "For real? Glad I got some cash on me."

"I'll pass," I say. "Trying to get my finances together so I can get my own ride instead of depending on my brother."

Suddenly my phone starts to blow up with multiple text notifications.

NEZZIE

Hey

So glad we connected again (3 hearts)

I missed you

Are you free?

U wanna come over?

I'm surprised Nezzie contacted me. She seemed uninterested in getting together when I saw her at the store yesterday. Now she's like the Nezzie I used to date. When she is high energy her texts come through like rapid bullets.

ME

What up Nez. Glad you got in touch with me. I'm at work right now. Not done until 11:30pm

NEZZIE

That's ok

I'll wait

I cooked oxtail

You love oxtail right?

ME

GTFOH, hell yes!

See you at midnight

NEZZIE

Ok
Can't wait
Can you bring some Blow?
I really really want some right now

"Yo Lance, can you hook a brother up with a gram and I'll pay you on Thursday?" I ask.

"What happened to getting your finances together?" Lance grins.

"Booty call. Bae's asking for Blow."

"I only got enough cash for myself. Sorry."

Adam says, "I got you Sim. But your ass better e-transfer me back Thursday morning."

I grin, "No doubt. Thanks brah."

ME

Yeah I'll bring some

NEZZIE

YASSS!!!

[Image]

See you later (kiss emoji)

Nezzie sends me a photo of her posing in front of the bathroom mirror wearing only a purple bra and thong panties. The extra meat on her booty from the last time we dated has me aroused. 11:30pm can't arrive any sooner.

New job, sexy boss, powder, and hooking up with an old flame. Other than my sister-in-law getting harassed on video, it's been a damn good week so far.

15

DARIAN

It's been a rough week physically and emotionally for me, Jessica and our friends. However, I'm thankful for Sunday. Although we work six days a week, we attend church even though we have the ultimate excuse to stay home and recuperate. But Jessica and I believe that if it wasn't for the Lord, we wouldn't be in this improving financial situation, so our family feels privileged to attend His house to worship and be encouraged.

I serve as an usher and help with hospitality while Jessica works with the Children's Ministry during Sunday service. It feels great to serve despite my fatigue, but it's greater to hear a powerful message by Pastors Marvin and Tammy, and it's on-point regarding what I want God to do in my life this year.

The service is almost complete, and I notice that during the offering Simon and Tracey step onto the stage with the Pastors. Right away, I believe it's about the horrible hate video. But how are they going to address it to the congregation?

"God bless you for being obedient and generous in your giving," Pastor Marvin begins. "Before we give the benediction, I brought up Simon and Tracey."

I cheer along with several other people in the congregation.

"Yes, for those who cheered, they know that this is one of our great new couples at Faith Worship Tabernacle. Great couple with two beautiful kids- twin kids. And they are also joining us on the Church Cruise which is going to be awesome!"

Simon smiles, "Can't wait."

"Yes, it's gonna be great. Now many of you probably don't know that Tracey is a police officer in the GTA. And as a female officer and a person of color, Tracey encounters acts of racism on a regular basis, correct me if I'm wrong?"

"No, it's true," Tracey agrees.

"And just this week a horrible video was released which shows Officer Tracey arresting a well-known multi-millionaire investor and he commits an act of hate towards her. It was absolutely disgusting! We aren't showing the video or sharing the link because we respect and admire this couple. Faith Worship Tabernacle, our God hates racism!"

"AMEN!" says the congregation.

"We should all have a zero tolerance for any hate speech or acts against someone because of their ethnicity or skin color. We need to see others as God sees us, and God is Love, amen?"

"Amen," I say with the crowd.

"So I want us to pray for protection over Tracey and her family. Harvest, if each of you can stretch your hands towards the Harrisons, Pastor Tammy is going to lead us in prayer."

Pastor Tammy says, "Lord, we thank you for Simon and Tracey and leading them to Faith Worship Tabernacle. Right now, we thank you for Tracey and her dedication and hard work as a police officer. We thank you for her service. Lord, we ask you for a hedge of protection over Tracey, that you keep her safe from harm and danger. We ask that when Tracey is involved with those who express hate that you remind her that you love her and always want the best for her. We pray for protection and success over Simon, Symon, and Symone as well. We thank you for the great things you're about to do in their lives. In Jesus' name, and everybody said-"

"AMEN!" we shout and clap with joy.

I'm overwhelmed with joy but I hold back my tears. I invited Simon to attend church in July of last year. He came without Tracey because she was on an assignment. The twins absolutely loved the Kids program, which encouraged Simon to return the following week with Tracey, and she loved the service. They accepted salvation the week after and now they are regular attendees.

Simon invited Skittles in August and now he attends more often. Skittles and I connected right away and it's great that all three of us attend the same church and workplace.

"So Simon," Jessica asks, "has that kid said anything to you since you threatened him?"

My wife and I, the Harrisons and Skittles are in the lobby chatting after church, taking our time to leave the premises.

"Nope," Simon says. "He's not even going to discuss it with the Union cuz he knows he wouldn't get far, especially with the Union District Rep being a person of color."

I say, "You did a good job not choking him out."

"Right?" Jessica says. "It's amazing to see how you both are holding it together."

"Funny you say that Jess," Tracey says. "I don't know how we held it together last year without God. Maybe God knew if this situation came up without Him taking control in our lives, I may have had a mental breakdown."

Simon adds, "And I may have been on my way to rehab."

"And how would that have affected our kids? Only God knows."

"I'm still learning about how God operates," Skittles says. "To be real, my faith level isn't anywhere close to where y'all are at. I still have a lot of questions."

I say, "Just keep coming every week, read His word and pray bro. Stay connected."

"I'm trying. There's a purpose for my life, but I just don't know what it is yet."

"You'll find it Skittles," Jessica says. "There's always a reason why we go through what we go through."

"Speaking of going through, my stomach is going through real hunger pains right now," Simon says. "Trace, you ready?"

"Yep," Tracey says while rolling her eyes. "You and your belly. We're going to his parents for dinner. They insisted on having us over today, for multiple reasons."

"All I want is my Dad's beef brisket. It's out of this world insanely good."

"Shoot," I say with envy. "Dinner at home is a simple baked chicken, macaroni pie and peas and rice."

"What? I'll take either dinner right now," Skittles says. "But I'm about to install some brakes for a lady from work, in hopes that if I do a dope job, she'll recommend me to others who need auto repair."

"Nuttin' wrong with that side hustle." I say.

"Yeah, and I ain't got a family yet so I got the spare time." Skittles grins as he leaves the building.

"I didn't smell any food cooking before we left for church," Jessica says to me as we drive away.

"It's not done yet," I admit. "The meat is seasoned, just gotta put it in the oven. Macaroni pie will only take an hour, and the rice-"

"Stop right there. You mean we, your wife and four kids, have to wait over an hour to have dinner when we're hungry now?"

"I'm just trying to save some-"

"We're getting takeout. I don't want to wait one or two hours for dinner when my body is in pain from work. Let's get takeout, then I'm taking a muscle relaxer and Tylenol, and I'm resting for the remainder of today. We work six days a week, so today needs to be stress-free."

"You're right hun. Takeout it is."

I'm being insensitive towards Jessica's health. It bothers me greatly that she has to endure so much physical pain just so we can get ahead in our finances.

16

TRACEY

"Dad, the food was amazing," I say to my father-in-law as he gathers up the plates from the dinner table.

"Thank you," Steve Harrison says. "Like always, take some food home with you. How are the kitchen renovations going?"

"It's looking great. Should be done in a couple of days. I'm actually looking forward to doing some cooking again."

"And when will that be darling?" Theresa Harrison says with a serious grin. "You and Simon work so much and you only had three days off during the Christmas break."

"I'll be off for three weeks in March. Two weeks on a Middle Eastern cruise with our church and one week at home. Can't wait."

Theresa and I have a unique relationship. She never liked the fact that her stepson married a cop, but we have two strong things in common- we are both Black women and married to White men. So, Theresa feels it's her obligation to not just be a mother-in-law, but to explain the ups and downs of an interracial marriage. As strong Black women, we have bumped heads numerous times, but I love and appreciate Theresa. She keeps everything one hundred, and she loves my husband like he is her biological son. As a result, I have a high level of respect for her.

Simon enters the dining room from the kitchen with pecan pie and vanilla ice cream. Steve is putting Netflix on the TV so his grandkids can watch a movie.

"So Tracey," my father-in-law asks, "did that sonofabitch apologize for-"

"Steve! Watch your language, the kids are in the room!" Theresa snaps.

"Oh! Sorry kids, Papa was just mumbling. Did that scum of a human being apologize to you?"

"Not in person Dad. It was a formal statement through his lawyer. O'Malley is also claiming mental health issues as the reason for his racial outburst and will probably use it as defense for a lesser sentence."

"That's bull- sorry you can't use a freaking mental health issue as an excuse for hate and pedophilia! Some of these Georgetown folks are unbelievable."

Simon asks, "Brings back memories, Pop?"

"It still bothers me to this day and I'm almost seventy. Lived in Georgetown my entire childhood life, up until the first three years with your late mother and I never had a problem with the community. The moment Theresa and I moved into a new home in Georgetown, we got death threats in my mailbox and the home phone telling up to move out. Theresa was getting mean stares and workers following her in the grocery store, wondering and asking why she has a four-year old White boy with her. All hell broke loose in their minds when they found out Theresa wasn't my nanny.

Theresa says, "I would take you to the playground and other ladies would ask 'How long have you been in Canada, because your English is so clear.' 'How long have you been working for Mr. Harrison?' Then as soon as I told them that I'm Steve's wife they either shut up or talk about how great Linda was. Don't get me wrong, I'm sure she was a fabulous woman, but they spoke about Linda to make me feel as if I was way below her class."

I shake my head in amazement, as I always do when my in-laws share their adventures as an interracial couple.

Simon says, "Wow Mom, I never heard that part of the story before. That's crazy."

"It is, right?" Theresa says. "At that point I told your father I wasn't going for groceries or the park unless he was with me, not because I was scared but I was tired of putting up with their sh-."

"Theresa!" Steve snaps.

"Oh please the kids didn't hear me. They reacted more to you saying 'Theresa!'" she says with her best impression of Steve.

I grin as he rolls his eyes in disagreement.

"Simon, Tracey, I don't think that everyone in Georgetown is a racist," Steve says, "but there are a trio of families in that town that have spewed hate for years- the O'Malley's, the Fishers, and the Newmans. I don't trust anybody with those last names at all. Moving out of Georgetown was probably the best decision of my life."

Theresa coughs.

"Best decision after marrying you, my Nubian queen," Steve smiles.

"So, we leave Georgetown to a more friendly city, and I got hired by Sutton to work in the HR office. My God Tracey, the amount of fakeness and hating I received from White ladies who admired my husband was incredible. That didn't bother me as much as the racism that took place behind my back. Back in the early 1980s, when every employee had to go to the bank to cash their paycheck, I was in the line waiting for a teller and my co-worker Emily is behind me. We do the usual fake small talk, and it was during that time when I noticed a check in her hand. It was almost two hundred dollars more than mine and she worked less hours than me."

Steve says, "Oh I remember that day you found out. I was furious and ready to raise hell to her manager, but Theresa stopped me."

Simon asks, "Why's that Mom? I mean you've told me the reason before but I didn't fully understand."

I've also explained the reason to Simon, but sometimes a spouse needs to hear it from someone else.

Theresa says, "Simon, if your father spoke for me and they fixed the situation, it wouldn't be for racial equality. They would've only done it as a favor for a White man. I had to speak to my manager. They had to hear of their intentional action from the only Black female employee in the office. I told my manager that he had to make my pay equal with Emily or I would expose them to the media, which was only TV or newspaper in the mid-eighties. He knew I was a damn good employee who took the HR department from good to great, so he made the pay adjustment. It didn't happen right away, and I bothered his ass every week until it happened.

Guys, I did this in 1986, long before all this social media stuff. If you want to see racial equality in your community and workplace, and I'm talking to you and Simon, you've got to bring the noise. If you don't bring the noise, you can't expect change."

Immediately when Theresa says "bring the noise" my mind thought of the old school Hip-Hop song. "Turn it up," I sing.

"Bring the noise!" Simon and I say together.

"That's a song?" Theresa asks.

"Public Enemy, Mom," Simon replies.

"Oh. Ok then."

Steve says, "Your mother doesn't like Rap. I know that tune. Original track, 1987 on *Nation of Millions* and the remix with Anthrax on the *Apocalypse 91'* album."

"Impressive knowledge Dad," I grin.

"Smoked some good weed with PE music back in the day."

I shake my head as I hear the front door open. My brother-in-law is here.

"Do I see Symon and Symone?" Simeon yells.

"Uncle Simmy!" the twins shout as they get up from the sofa to give him a hug. They love his energy and willingness to act silly.

"Hey Trace," Simeon says as we hug. "How are you? So sorry you had to go through that mess on video. O'Malley needs to burn in hell. You good though?"

"I'm getting through it by God's help day by day, thanks for asking," I say. "How's work going at Sutton?"

"Sweet, couldn't have asked for a better first week. I'm finally at a place in my life where I feel financially comfortable."

"Don't get too comfortable cuz you need to be saving up for your own damn place," Theresa says.

Steve adds, "And your own damn ride too."

Simon starts laughing out loud, as if he knew this conversation was coming.

Rolling his eyes, Simeon says, "Gimme time, my dear parents. Speaking of ride, Mom can I take your car this afternoon? I got-"

"Didn't you just come home? You barely took off your boots coming from who knows where and you wanna go out again?" Theresa responds. "Eat some food, relax a minute, and play with your niece and nephew."

"I will Mom. I ain't rushing, still gotta wait until she comes home from church."

I ask, "Oh nice you're dating a church girl?"

Simeon grins, "Uh, yeah you can say that."

I see my husband shake his head as he looks at his little brother. He obviously knows something about Simeon that's bothering him.

It's so great to spend a day with the family after a rough week. I really need more time off, but I'm grateful for what I can get. God will help me go through the stress of work until it's time to go on my real vacation.

17

SKITTLES

As I drive to Donna's house to pick her up, I'm wrestling with an important decision. There is no doubt that I'm obsessed with making money. I have some immediate financial goals that I can't avoid, but emotions are getting in the way.

Donna dropped off her Sutton SUV on my driveway, but instead of waiting at my house I took her to the nearby shopping mall. It only took me ninety minutes to assemble the brakes, which pleased Donna very much. Even though she's a single mother and recently divorced, Donna has a confident personality, which makes me more attracted to her whenever she speaks.

As she comes out of the mall towards my ride, Donna gives me a big smile and I grin back. I don't know if I'm interested in dating her, but I feel more confident with the news I'm ready to give her.

"No!" she cries. "Skittles, I gotta pay you for your labor!"

"Hear me out," I say. "I've only been at Sutton for a week so I don't know many people yet, even though many know me because of my washroom drama."

"You've handled the ridicules really well, and that's why-"

"Hold on, lemme finish. You brought me the parts which made it quicker for me to install the brakes. Also, I enjoy mechanical work way more than working on the line. I need a side hustle outside of work and you're my first customer. If you tell just a few people that I'm a certified mechanic that's ready and available, clients from word of mouth will more than make up for this Pro Bono."

"Ok, I have no problem doing that. Thank you Skittles."

"You're welcome. My pleasure."

"I'll definitely get you more customers. You need to make up for the lessor wage you new hires make."

"I know right?"

Although we are both assembly line workers, I make twenty-one dollars an hour while Donna makes thirty-five. It's not fair, but that's what I must start with as a new employee based on the most recent contract between Sutton and the Union.

"I still feel like I owe you something," Donna says. "Lemme at least take you out for dinner."

This threw me off. I didn't expect Donna to make the first move. "My spouse won't be happy about that," I lie.

"Oh please, you're a terrible liar," Donna smiles. "If you were married you wouldn't give me free service. And I see you grinning. Yes, I think you look good too."

"Ok, are you usually this straight forward?"

"Usually. I'm a proud feminist who knows what I want and will not hesitate to speak my mind. That's probably why my ex-husband and I don't get along anymore."

We arrive back to my house and Donna steps into her vehicle after I show her the new brake pads on her ride. As she starts the engine, she says, "Thanks again. Now where do you wanna go for dinner?"

"No idea," I reply. "I'll let you know at work tomorrow."

"If you mention any burrito joint, the deal's off."

I laugh, "Definitely not. See ya later."

My grin is in full effect as she drives away. Yes, I'm feeling the single soccer mom, but the grin goes away when I see my nosy mother staring through the living room window.

18

AUDRE

It's a new week and I'm hoping for zero drama, but it seems to follow me like my last name. The first two hours at work involved a work refusal on the Door line because of an unknown toxic smell from one of the auto parts. A middle-aged man complained that he was dizzy as a result of the odor. He walked off the line and pressed the stop button. Then, we were down for over two hours until the smell went away.

There's only two hours left in the evening shift and I need an adrenaline rush. I place my BT buds in my ears and play an eighties Soul Disco mix. I've only been getting four to five hours of sleep, mainly because of my withdrawal from sleeping pills. That was my crutch for several weeks. I would be wide awake in my bed dealing with lower back pain, stressing about bills, stressing about my sons, thinking about Hank, and all the crazy mess that's going on with my friends. But now when I'm sleepless I just smoke a joint and it's been working. It still doesn't take away my stress though.

As I'm working on the Door Line, I'm observing the student working on my left. Carolyn seems like she's staring at nothing in particular while using a long power tool and completing her job. I think she's either sick or high.

"Carolyn?" I ask her as I pause my music. "Carolyn, are you ok hun?"

She nods without looking at me. I continue to eye her while I'm working. Minutes later, I notice that Carolyn's left leg is twitching. Not good. I take out my earbuds and yell "SANDY!", who is my team leader.

Suddenly I hear a loud bang on the floor. Carolyn drops the power tool because her entire body is now twitching. She's having a seizure, which causes Carolyn's head to hit the sharp corner of the door and she falls to the pavement.

"HELP!" I yell in panic. "SOMEBODY STOP THE LINE!"

Sandy runs to the nearest button and slams it. Grabbing her walkie-talkie, she says, "Trent, come to 1057R. We have an emergency. Worker is down!"

Carolyn is twitching but now blood is gushing from her forehead. My new friend Hardeep is already on the phone calling the medical office to bring some help. I lift Carolyn's head and place it on my lap.

"She was just in a staring trance for like a half hour," I explain to Sandy. "Then when her leg was shaking, I called you but it was too late."

"We can't control the time when a seizure shows up," Sandy says. "She just needs to get to a hospital."

My supervisor Trent rushes to the scene and asks what happened. I explain the story again.

"We need medical here right now, Door Line 1057R," Trent says through his walkie-talkie.

Sandy says, "We already called medical."

"Ok. Sandy, take over from Audre please."

I say, "I'm ok, I got her until medical arrives."

"That's alright Audre, I'm just gonna move Carolyn away from the doors until medical gets here," Sandy says while taking the thin college student from me. Another worker places a wet rag on her head to control the bleeding. Trent is yelling for an absentee replacement to cover Carolyn's job.

"Ok, here we go," Trent says as he releases the start button.

The line is moving. I'm in disbelief.

"What the hell? Why is the line moving?" I cry.

Trent says, "Medical is on their way. We gotta keep the line moving."

"Are you serious? We got a girl who's in a critical condition and all you care about is making cars? Stop the line!"

Other workers are complaining with me as well. I'm ready to do another work refusal.

"Audre, we have a quota to reach and because the line was down for half the shift already, we gotta-"

"STOP THE DAMN LINE!"

"No!"

I walk away from my job towards the button, slightly pushing Trent away to stop the line again. Now I'm staying in front of the button.

"What are you doing Audre? MOVE AWAY!"

Trent tries to make a gesture to move me, but I lift my hand.

I warn, "If you touch me, we gonna have a problem."

Hardeep shouts, "I'm calling the Union for you Audre!"

Trent says, "Union can't do anything. You're on probation so I can fire you right now!"

I say, "Do what you have to do, but I'm staying here until Carolyn is in good hands."

The supervisor lifts his hands and walks away, looking angry and scared because management will be looking for answers. But I don't care. As a widow, I am very passionate about people getting the medical care that they need, even if it means losing my job. At the same time, I can't afford to get fired but I'm not backing down.

Within minutes of my work refusal, the entire Door Line crew are in the area. So is Johnny, my Union Rep, Kareem Chan, the District Rep for our shift, a couple of health and safety reps and some management heads. Because I'm covering the button I can't see how Carolyn is doing because a crowd is surrounding her.

Simon comes by, observes the crowd for a minute, and then he approaches me. "My friend," he grins, "You've only been on the line for a week and you're already making noise."

"You know me," I say, "I don't put up with mess for a long time. Who cares about a freaking car when someone's life is in jeopardy?"

"It's all about the bottom line for Sutton. However, medical will be here in about two minutes. I saw them driving down the main aisle."

"About time."

Johnny comes toward me and says, "Trent is whining how you pushed him over to stop the line. I don't believe him. What really happened?"

I explain the entire story from Carolyn's early signs to the present moment. A few others were also listening including Kareem, who is a friend from high school. Suddenly, the attention is on me, even though medical has arrived and places Carolyn on a carry bed.

"Your call to action today was admirable," says Johnny. "We need strong advocates like you in the Union."

Kareem laughs. "Be careful what you ask for, Johnny. Dre is stubborn as hell. Jokes aside though, she would be incredible in the Union because she brings the noise."

I smile with Kareem but it's short lived. Trent is storming towards me after talking with a circle of managers. Behind him is a well-known person in the plant according to the workers staring at him.

Simon says, "Whoa, Vito Martino is coming this way."

I ask, "Who's he?"

"The Plant Manager."

Trent yells, "Ok, everybody to your stations, we're starting the line in two minutes!"

The Plant Manager says, "Audre, I'm Vito Martino, the Plant Manager of Sutton Assembly. I appreciate the effort you took in an emergency like this, but you can't overrule a supervisor's decision when it comes to starting or stopping the line."

I say, "With all due respect sir, the medical staff wasn't here yet. When you see someone injured in a sports match do they not restart the game once the athlete is carted away?"

"Yes. But while medical was on its way your team leader was off the line taking care of her."

"So that means it's back to business as usual? If that girl was your daughter would you care if Sutton builds 450 cars a shift?"

"I understand. Hopefully something like this won't happen again."

Vito walks away without answering the question. Did "something like this" mean my behavior or the workplace injury? Chills start to set in. Whatever the answer may be, the real question is whether or not I will still be a Sutton employee at the end of the day.

19

SIMON

I arrive at my parents' house a few minutes early to pick up Simeon. While I wait in the driveway, I decide to send my boy Kareem a text. As a District Representative he would know about the current status of Audre.

ME

Hey, did you get a chance to discuss the line incident with management? Audre is nervous as hell that she's gonna lose her job.

KAREEM

I spoke to our Plant Chairperson who spoke to Vito. Because it was an emergency and Audre showed compassion for the injured student, she won't get fired and it won't be held against her during her probation. If she keeps a clean record until the end of her 90 days.

"Praise the Lord," I say as I respond to the text.

ME

Awesome. Thanks bro. How's the girl doing?

KAREEM

Has a concussion but she's going to be fine in a few weeks.

ME

(thumbs up emoji)

"What up big bro?" Simeon grins as he enters my vehicle. "Ready for an action-packed, drama-filled shift? Sutton crazy always going on!"

"Too much crazy," I answer. "This month couldn't start off anymore crazy. I hope 2020 gets better than this."

"How's Tracey handling everything?"

"My wife is tough as nails bro. Doing cases, dealing with the media, radio interviews, article features, then coming home to be a mother and wife. Tracey really needs a vacation. I can't wait to go on the cruise."

"She deserves it. Both of y'all do. Damn I wish I could join you. I love cruises."

"I'm so looking forward to it," I grin. "But we're going with our church family. If you came along, you couldn't drink."

"Come again? GTFOH, no drinking? Nobody at your church drinks? How you go on a cruise and not have some liquor?"

"Hah, I guess I'll find out. I'm still trying to get used to life without a lil' drink, but by God's grace I'm pushing through."

"Meh. No buzz on a vacay? I'll pass. Hey bro, can you drop me off at my friend's crib after work?"

My mind alarm goes off. Whenever Simeon says "my friend", he doesn't want to share their name to avoid judgment. But I have a feeling it's Nezzie.

"Is it Nezzie?" I ask.

"Yeah," he answers but notices my screw face expression. "What?"

"I can't believe you're seeing her again after all the misery y'all went through together."

"I don't know man. Misery loves company. Look, I know the girl is bipolar but she's on meds now and doing much better."

Simeon didn't look at me when he said that, so I feel like he's hiding more information.

"That's good to know," I say. "So, what do you guys do when you're together?"

Now he looks at me. "Whatcumean what do we do? We're a couple, we do couple things."

"But isn't Nezzie a Christian now? What do you guys do now compared to when y'all dated before?"

"Where the hell you going with this Simon?" he asks after what seems like a thirty second pause.

"When y'all get together now, do you get the old Nezzie or the new Nezzie? The old meaning you guys do what you enjoy doing, or the new Nezzie meaning y'all do what Nezzie enjoys doing now?"

"What does Nezzie like to do now?"

"I don't know, you tell me. Alright, you know the difference between the old me and the new me by now right? The old Simon was an alcoholic. New Simon stopped drinking. Old Simon easily got depressed and angry. New Simon still gets angry, but I put my trust in God. See where I'm going with this?"

"Yeah, but Nezzie ain't you. Me and her are cool, so stop tripping. If you don't wanna drop me to her house, all you gotta do is say so and not go into some religious rant!"

I shake my head because Simeon is being stubborn and he isn't hearing what I have to say. Perhaps if I drop him to his GF after work it will give me a better chance to explain why they shouldn't be together.

"My bad," I say. "I can drop you to her place after work."

"Why? So you can try to lecture me some more about this? Nah man I'm good. I'll just contact my friend Uber and pay him a few dollars. At least Uber doesn't judge my ass."

"Fine. Suit yourself."

We drive for a minute in silence before I decide to release my thought filter. "Not judging you Sim. But I know your idea of fun: drinking, smoking, whatever gets you a good high. If you say Nezzie is a believer now, that means she shouldn't be doing the stuff you like to do. So, when you get together, do you influence Nezzie, or does she influence you? If you're the influencer then- never mind, forget it."

"Then what?" Simeon snaps. "I'll bring her down to my level? Suddenly you care about Nezzie's well-being? Nezzie's too good for me because she's a Christian and I'm not?"

I want to say yes to piss him off, but Simeon is already hot.

"Look, all I'm saying is that-"

"Nah, forget whatever the hell you gotta say. Whatever I do is never good enough for you, Mom or Dad. Damn, I hate how you White boys think y'all are perfect with relationships because you have a Black woman. I get a Black woman and you wanna complain how she ain't right for me!"

I laugh at his ridiculous rant. "What the hell? How is race a part of this discussion? I don't give a damn what race Nezzie is, I'm talking about salvation. Be a reason for her elevation, not her downfall."

"Downfall? Whoever said Nezzie's on a downfall? And why the hell would I be the reason for her downfall? You're just talking crap bro. I need to get outta this whip before I do or say something I regret."

"Go ahead, get out. Your ass could never handle criticism anyway."

"Maybe it's because it's coming from you who thinks he's a White boy who never makes as much mistakes as his little Black stepbrother!"

"You tripping bro, my kids are black so why would I think that?" I yell as he slams my door and walks away.

Simeon and I have a rollercoaster relationship. He's always been more free-spirited like our father, and I have been the more disciplined like my stepmom. However, because I'm White and Simeon is mixed, he often tries to bring up the race card whenever I offer advice. For him to always think I look down on him because he's half-black is asinine, and it pisses me off every time he brings it up.

An incoming call from Tracey appears on the screen just as I'm about to turn off the truck. I have a good amount of time to spare before work starts so I keep the vehicle on and answer the Bluetooth. "Hey luv."

Tracey says, "Hey babes, how are you?"

"My brother gets on my damn nerves," I answer before explaining the argument that just took place.

"You are far from a racist, babe," she says, "but you need to stop lecturing Simeon. Just pray for him and let God deal with him like how God dealt with you. You're his older brother that he's been envious of for a long time. Someone who's not close to him can say everything you told him about Nezzie, and Sim will probably receive it better. Prayer works, so let God have his way with your brother."

"You're right," I agree with hesitancy. My wife has a gift of making sense out of my nonsense. "How's your day going?"

"Great. You are now talking to the new Detective Sergeant of Halton Police Department."

My eyes grow big with joy. "Oh my God, congratulations babe! Wow, that's amazing. They told you much sooner than I thought they would."

"I know right? The department wanted this position filled ASAP and Liam told me that I was the clear-cut choice to fill the position once he becomes Sergeant Major next week."

"Trace, I'm so happy for you. Look how God works! Our Pastors prayed for you at church after the O'Malley incident and two days later you get promoted!"

"I'm so glad you're excited for me babes."

"Why wouldn't I be?" I ask, feeling a little confused. "This is what you want, right?"

"Yes, but this means possibly more hours away from you and the kids and-"

"Look Trace, yes I know it's a more demanding position, but you are living your dream of fighting for justice and I'm more at peace with it since the church prayed for you on Sunday. The Lord will never give us more than we can handle. I'm good if you're good. You good?"

"I'm great. It looks like the scripture Jeremiah 29:11 really holds true."

"What does it say?"

"For I know the plans I have for you, says the Lord. Plans for good and not disaster, to give you a future and a hope. That has been my go-to verse ever since that man humiliated me on video. I'm still far from being over it and I'm battling anger issues about it, but God is so faithful. He's faithful to me, to you, our marriage and our family. I'm so thankful right now. God is so good!"

"Yes He is. We need to celebrate this accomplishment with a get-together party next-"

"No," she interrupts. "Nothing big, Simon. We're still saving money for our cruise."

"Nothing big, I promise. We'll do it at our house. Make use of our brand-new renovated kitchen. We gotta celebrate God's goodness to us and..."

"And what?"

"Your promotion doesn't affect our time off for the cruise, right?"

She laughs, "You kidding? Hell no! I become Detective Sergeant after we come back. There's no way we aren't going on the Church Cruise!"

"Man, I can't wait. And I'm going to start planning the party-"

"Social, Simon."

"Social, got it. Oh, I just got a message from the Union about Audre. She's not going to get fired for stopping the line."

"Good, thank God. She and I are so overdue to hang out. Hey, I gotta finish up some paperwork before I go home. Talk to you later babes. Love you."

20

SKITTLES

"Cheers to getting through your first two weeks," Donna says as we toast our beer mugs. It's late Saturday night and she kept her promise of treating me to dinner.

"Cheers," I grin. "This is nice, I appreciate you taking me out."

"My pleasure. You must be worth it for me to eat this late."

"My bad. Working afternoons got me eating big at one in the morning."

"That was me during my first five years at Sutton. I was wider and overweight but now I look and feel sexy, thanks to intermittent fasting."

"Wow, good for you. So, when do you start and stop eating?"

"I start at noon and stop at 8 pm. But if I know in advance that I'm going out to eat, all rules are off. So tonight I'm having steak!"

Work was done at 11:18 pm which didn't give me time to go home and change. I brought extra clothes and freshened up in the washroom. I assume Donna did the same because we both arrive at Sammy's Gastropub before midnight. She caught my attention with the red lipstick and hoop earrings. It makes me wonder if something else is going to happen past dinner.

Donna says, "You've really made a name for yourself in the last two weeks on our shift."

"Yeah, for good and bad reasons," I laugh. "No need to recap the bad."

"Nope, no need. But the last two days were two of the most enjoyable days I've ever had on Engine Line."

Donna is referring to me singing and dancing while operating on the assembly line. It was suggested in my orientation class that while on probation, new hires should not use earbuds or headphones while working because the supervisor could use it as a reason to not hire me permanently. But after a week and a half, the job got very boring and everyone around me had their earbuds on. So I placed on my BT earbuds and got in my musical zone. Shortly thereafter, I was singing out loud and entertaining everyone who heard me. Now I was known as a mechanic, "S--ttles" because of the washroom drama, and a karaoke singer.

"For real?" I ask with surprise. "That's how I always listen to music- at home, my car or at work. It brings me joy."

"The look that Brad gave you the first time he saw you singing was priceless. Our shift goes so much better when he's frustrated or embarrassed."

We go into a variety of topics before and after we get our steak entrees. Donna says that there is a certain "aura" that she feels when I am around. Although she used a new age term, I know she's talking about the Godly joy in me. I know that I'm not a strong believer and I often worry about money, but the three things I try to do consistently: my daily devotion from the church app on my phone, five minutes of prayer, and going to church every Sunday. I am very far from where God wants me to be, but my life could be so much worse without Him.

This topic leads to me opening about my past and present personal life. I got married at twenty-two and divorced at twenty-four. It was my fault; I had an affair with my high school sweetheart who was also married. It was the biggest mistake of my life. I told her that I would leave my wife if she left her husband. She didn't fulfill her promise because she thought it made more sense for her to stay married to her husband who's a rich real estate agent.

Presently, I'm divorced and living with my parents. When I moved back home, I was dependent on them until I got back on my feet financially. Now, it's the other way around. My mother is on disability and my father owns a convenience store that struggles to pay their bills. I was helping to pay their mortgages and it was draining my income. My stress level was higher at my previous mechanic job because my former boss was underpaying me. That's why I'm so thankful for Sutton giving me an honest weekly pay.

"I'll do what I can to get you more clients," Donna says with sincerity.

"I appreciate it, even though you've already done plenty," I say. "So tell me, why are you divorced?"

"I'll keep the story short because it's still fresh. It only happened six months ago."

"Are you still bitter about it?"

"I am, but I keep cool about it most of the time. My ex works at FCA aka Chrysler and we work opposite shifts as that someone is always with the kids. He stopped communicating, opened a separate bank account for his paycheck and our marriage kept going downhill. The last straw was when I finished work early during day shift. I purposely didn't inform him that I was coming home early. Then, I saw an unknown car in the driveway and it belonged to another woman."

Her story makes me feel like a dog for my cheating past. "At that point what did you do?"

"Waited until the thot left. Went inside and swung a fist across his face and threw his clothes out the window. What did your wife do to you?"

"I told her I cheated. She threw some porcelain cups at my head and told me to get out. So I did."

"Hmmm," Donna ponders. "So, if your high school sweetheart came in here right now and said she was divorced from her husband and wants you back, would you take her?"

That question re-occurred in my mind at least once a day for several years after my divorce. I'm curious as to why Donna wants to know. Would my answer determine if I'm boyfriend material? Is her mind already made up that I'm a dog?

I answer, "It's been fifteen years since my divorce. My high school sweetheart lied to me and as a result she kept her marriage while I lost mine. That showed me that we weren't meant to be together. I've moved on, and it took me a long time to get to this point. So, my answer is no."

"Ok," she says while taking a sip of beer. Donna doesn't buy my answer.

"You don't believe me?"

"I'm not sure," Donna admits, "but I'm pretty bitter about men right now. Getting into another relationship is the last thing I wanna do now."

"I understand."

"But I do want you to come over after we're done here. My kids are with their dad this weekend."

I suddenly feel warm and horny. Not knowing what to say next, I put a piece of steak in my mouth and chew. I have to attend church in the morning. I don't have to, but I want to. Because sex is already on my mind I must quickly rebuke or encourage the thought. Help me Lord!

"I'd love to," I say after swallowing my food. "You live far from here?"

"Only twenty minutes away. With your long pause I thought you were going to refuse."

"I was just surprised that you want me to come over after saying you don't want a-"

"It's just one evening. No commitment."

"No commitment. So... how's your steak?"

"So damn delicious."

I said yes to going to her house because I know Eddie Persaud. It's either I sleep with Donna and go to church the next day. Or I could refuse, go home and jerk off, then go to church the next day. Both options will lead me to repentance.

While I'm telling a funny story about something that took place at my old job, Donna's attention is towards the restaurant entrance and her smile disappears.

"Get the hell outta here," she grumbles.

"What's going on?"

"My ex-husband is here. His ass is supposed to be at his home with my kids."

I turn around and see two men wearing baseball caps with a couple of ladies by their side, laughing and enjoying themselves. Donna pulls out her phone and sends a text while staring at one of the guys as if she wants to kill him.

"My text to him said, *Why is your ass not home with our kids? Look to your right.*" she says to me.

Sure enough, the man looks in our direction and begins to frown. He heads toward our table after telling his crew he needs to be excused.

"Of all the pubs in this city, what are the chances of us being at the same one?" he asks while staring at both of us.

Donna answers, "It would be zero if you were home with them right now Dylan!"

"My mother is at the apartment, plus they're sleeping anyway. What's the big deal?"

"The big deal is that you get your kids for three days every two weeks and during your three days you still feel the need to be away from them."

Changing the subject, Dylan glares at me from head to toe and asks her, "Who is that?" like I wasn't at the table.

"This is Skit- Eddie, a friend from work."

I stretch out my hand but Dylan leaves me hanging like it was dirty.

He says, "Donna, can we talk about this privately? Parental stuff."

After letting out a huge sigh she says to me, "I'll be right back."

Donna and Dylan go out of the pub. I stare at the exit for a minute and then go back to finishing my food. The friends that are with Dylan are escorted to a booth. The white male in the baseball cap is staring at me as he sits down. It's a stare as if he knows who I am. Then the lady next to him takes off his cap to get his attention.

I gasp as I recall his familiar face. It's the officer that pulled me over twelve days ago. The cop that I couldn't report because I didn't know his badge number.

Now, I'm angry. The unnecessary search of my vehicle in the cold. Making me wait a half-hour in my car afterwards for a damn warning, knowing that I would almost be late for work. All of this because I was Driving While Black.

The more I want to approach him and let out my frustration, the more I consume my food and beverage. I just can't forgive him and move on from the incident.

"Oh, I can't stand him," Donna grumbles as she sits down, interrupting my angry thoughts. "And to think I have to deal with him until my youngest turns eighteen. You okay Skittles? What's wrong?"

"Who's the guy that came with your ex?"

Sucking her teeth, she says, "Oh. That's Tucker Mayfield, Dylan's longtime friend. I can't stand him either."

Donna turns around to see that Tucker is looking at me, gives a fake smile and wave. He does the same. "Why do you ask, you seen him before? He's a cop."

I say, "Yes, that's why he looks familiar."

"Hey, I know that I invited you over after this, but Dylan really pissed me off and now I'm tired. Raincheck?"

Music to my spiritual ears. "Of course. Before your ex came, this was a great time."

"I agree. You're fun to be around. Next time we are working on day shift and I don't have the kids, we'll do this again. No commitment."

"No commitment."

"And if that goes well, who knows? FWB perhaps?"

Friends With Benefits? I did promise God that the next person I date will be wifey material.

"Perhaps," I say. "We'll see."

Dylan and Tucker keep staring at me until we leave the gastropub. Tucker probably told him about pulling me over, to give him the notion that his children's mother is dating a criminal. I'm glad I know his name, now I can report about his behavior to the police department.

21

SIMEON

I had just completed my first two weeks of work on afternoon shift and I loved it. Wake up at noon, work from 3:30 to 11:30pm, then drink and get high until four in the morning. But now it's Sunday, my only day off until Monday when I switch to the morning shift. A 6:30am start is torture for me, which is why I agreed to meet up with Nezzie at noon so I can get my ass to bed early tonight.

Now that I'm getting a consistent pay every week, my dad is nicer with lending me the truck because I can afford to fill his tank. Before I left the driveway, I text Nezzie that I'm on my way. She replies *Ok my boo.* I give it a puzzling stare. She's calls me "baby", "sexy", "bae", and "Simmy Love" but never boo. But Nezzie is unpredictable sometimes and I love that about her.

I knock on her door while holding two bags of Chinese food. Nezzie opens and gives me a nervous smile.

"Hey bae. Brought some lunch," I smile while holding up the bags.

"Simmy, I-"

"You just can't leave her alone, can you?" says a man who appears behind Nezzie. It's her older brother who I met when we last dated.

"Keith! What's going on, how are-"

POW!

I feel a fist smash my nose and lips as I fall to the floor. Blood is running down my right nostril.

"Man, what the fu-"

I get up and see Nezzie's father in front of Keith.

"Simmy, I'm so sorry," Nezzie says in tears.

"Whatcu sorry for?" her dad snaps. "The only thing you should be sorry for is letting this junkie back in your life!"

I say, "Sir, Nezzie shouldn't be-"

"SHUT UP! You need to stay away from my daughter! Nezzie's life was going well before she connected back with you. Last Sunday, she came to church high! This Sunday she doesn't show up because she has a hangover. You're the reason why this is happening. You!"

This is only half the truth. Nezzie contacted me first after I gave her my number. She wanted to get back to her old ways. I helped her fulfill her desires. Now I wish I didn't.

"I care about your daughter sir."

"No you don't! You're a cancer to my daughter!"

Keith says, "Nezzie's roommate says the only time she calls you is when she's off her meds. What does that tell you?"

It tells me that I make her feel good. But it does remind me of when we reunited at the convenience store. Nezzie wasn't that happy to see me. She was on her meds.

"I'm the one who responded to your text," says her father. "I now have her phone. If you try to come over, I know the person in the apartment next door and she will call me if she sees you. This is your first and hopefully the last warning."

Nezzie is crying but she doesn't defend me. Her silence speaks volumes, but the medication is taking over her.

I drive away with my face in sheer pain, desperate for a pack of ice. But the bigger pain is realizing that Simon may be right. Damn, I really wanted to start something special with her.

22

TRACEY

Feb 1, 2020

"Babe, what vegan dishes are we having tonight?" I ask my husband as he is seasoning chicken for tonight's celebration dinner.

"Vegan dishes?" Simon asks. "Who's coming tonight that's vegan?"

"Simon, our Pastors are vegan. How are you going to invite Pastor Marvin and Tammy and not have anything for them to eat?"

"Well, I can put together a few vegetables to boil, make a salad and-"

"No, Simon! Rabbit food isn't the solution for a good vegan meal. I'm gonna run to Whole Foods and get some... why are you laughing?"

Simon is chuckling and it's making me more frustrated. The social is only three hours away and he promised to take care of everything, since it was his idea.

"I'm kidding luv. Mom is bringing two plant-based dishes and Audre is making a vegan mac and cheese. I told you I got this."

I let out a sigh of relief and grin as he kisses my cheek.

"Relax baby," he says. "This will be a great night because we're celebrating your success and nothing less."

To be honest, I don't really care for a party to celebrate my promotion to Detective Sergeant. January was a physically and emotionally draining month and if I can just relax with Simon and the kids on my day off, I'll be more than pleased. But Simon wants to do this and celebrating my success helps him to break any insecurities he still has of me being a cop. All I can say is prayer works. He is my number one supporter, and he hasn't returned to the liquor. God is so good.

The O'Malley drama hasn't gone away but it's starting to die down. I've had interviews on talk shows and magazines with a couple of speaking engagements lined up for Black History Month. God has opened doors for me to inspire and empower people through the Internet and in person, for which I'm truly grateful for the opportunities. Harpreet is reaping the benefits as well, being a role model for the Indian community.

Those are the only positive effects of the altercation. Georgetown is beginning to feel the financial downfall of O'Malley's businesses in the community, and some are blaming Harpreet and myself; forgetting that the multi-millionaire was arrested for distributing child porn. A few residents have thanked us for taking out the cancer in their town, but a few ignorant folks are saying that a Black and an Indian cop has caused havoc in their pre-dominantly White city. Add a few rape cases that we've been investigating, and it's been a rough three weeks. But there's a light at the end of the tunnel, because my vacation is less than five weeks away.

Audre is the first guest to arrive, one hour before the social to help with the food prep. I give her a hug like I haven't seen her in ten years.

"Damn I missed you girl, even though we text and video chat almost every day," Audre says.

"For real. So much is going on which makes us so busy. But we got some time now, let's chat before the others come through," I reply.

"Ok! Bring out the wine, let's catch up."

"Uh, I don't have any more wine, Dre."

"Girl, stop playing," Audre says while grabbing some wine glasses. "You always have wine."

"Not anymore. I told you already that Simon and I stopped drinking."

"Even on special occasions?"

"Yes Dre. But I got some blue mountain coffee."

"Girl, I don't want no damn coffee. How did you get through January without drinking?"

"I can't lie, it was hard. But I only made it through God's grace. How are the twins doing?"

Audre lets out a frustrating sigh. "Ok, get me some coffee."

We sit around the island in the kitchen and have a lengthy chat as Audre shares about Tristan and Terrell. "You know just like me Trace, twins can be so alike and so different."

I laugh, "That is so true. The way Symon and Symone handle situations are almost night and day."

"And that's been the case since their father died. Tristan gave up playing sports completely and is laser-focused on doing his absolute best in school. Hard-working like Hank was at his job. Tristan is all about excellence. He's sensitive, but still has Hank's stubbornness. It's only a "black or white" answer, never grey.

I'm really worried about Terrell though. He loves playing sports but doesn't give a damn about his grades. Mother instinct is telling me he's involved with something he doesn't want me to know about. He never wants to be home, stays out late and always smells like weed. Something ain't right, and I hope he's not doing the street life."

I ask, "You want me to arrange a GPS tracker on him?"

Her eyes light up. "I was gonna ask if you can do that, but not yet. I'm gonna peel Terrell like an onion, layer by layer until I get some answers."

"Ok, well let me know. You know Simon and I are always here for you girl."

"Thanks hun, and you know it's likewise for me. Damn, I'm learning to go through life better without Hank, but every day I miss him so much. I wish he was here to handle some of this."

Audre begins to weep as I give her a hug. "Dre, remember this: God will never give you more than you can handle."

"Well, He's definitely testing me. Me and Him aren't cool like that, not like He is with you."

I want to respond, but the doorbell is ringing. It's Jessica, Darian and their four children. Symon and Symone are excited because they love playing with their youngest daughter, Janiya.

"Thanks for coming guys," I say after Simon and I hug them.

Jessica says, "I wasn't going to miss this! We're so happy for your promotion."

"Audre, have you met Jessica and Darian yet? They're the ones who invited us to church. They both work-"

"I know, I know, we finally get to meet," Audre says as they greet. "I heard a lot about you two. Only good stuff of course."

"Likewise," Darian says, "from Simon and Skittles. Other people from work know you as the 'badass new hire who stopped the line.'"

Jessica adds, "That's all I was hearing that day, 'Oh, some new hire stopped the line and told off the Plant Manager!'"

Audre laughs. "I didn't tell off the Plant Manager. I did tell them that I wasn't moving from the start button until that girl received medical attention. At that point I didn't give a damn if they fired me or not."

"Well, props to you hun, and thank you. I needed that line stop cuz I was in a lot of pain that day."

"What area do you work, Jessica? You're still on probation?"

"Yeah, I'm almost done probation, about a month away. I'm on the Final Line. The job is repetitive and I've been in so much pain. I can't wait to take some weekends off after my ninety days are up. You work on the Door Line?"

"Yeah, it's crazy over there. The other day..."

I leave Audre and Jessica chatting as I go to the door to let in another guest. "Skittles! What up homie? Looking shinier than ever in your gold and purple jacket," I say as we hug.

"Yep. In honor of Kobe," Skittles says. "I was watching his videos all week. I just can't believe he's dead, it's so surreal."

"Very surreal. Losing a husband and a daughter in a helicopter crash must be so devastating for Vanessa and her girls. I've been praying for her all week. Kobe was legendary. Simon and I saw his last all-star game in Toronto, on lower-level seats."

"Hmph, I remember the envy I was feeling when Simon told me y'all had tickets. RIP Kobe and Gianna. Hey Trace, I found out the name of the cop who pulled me over and I filed a complaint. His name is Tucker Mayfield."

I told Skittles last week that I could find info on the officer if I have his name or badge number. "Tucker Mayfield. Do me a favor, text me the name and I'll do some digging when I go back to the office."

Our home is quickly filling up. Pastor Marvin and Tammy came through, followed by Simon's parents with Simeon, Harpreet and his female guest, and former Detective Sergeant now Sergeant Major Liam Anderson. Pastor Tammy prayed thanks for the food and now we're just enjoying each other's company. Everyone except Simeon, who went to the basement with the kids. Usually, he would be playing the X-Box One with them, but he's sitting in the sofa looking depressed as he scrolls through his phone.

I ask, "Hey bro, how come you're not having any food?"

He says, "I ate before I got here, so I'm not hungry. Congratulations, if I haven't told you already."

"Thank you. I'm actually surprised that you came, considering that you and your brother haven't been on good terms lately."

As long as I've known my brother-in-law, his conversations are always unfiltered. That's why I never beat around the bush when I talk to him.

"That's because I refuse to admit he was right. Again."

"About what?"

"The girl I was seeing. She's taking meds for her bipolar illness and goes to church. She wants to get with me when she's off the meds to get high and do the nasty- I mean other stuff. So, Simon told me that I need to do the stuff that makes Nezzie a better person when I'm with her."

"Instead of doing only what she wants to do."

"Exactly."

"And how's that working out for you?"

"It's not. Her family stopped me from seeing her because she went back to her old addictions after seeing me."

"Well Sim, it's not all your fault. When a woman wants something, she has two choices: do whatever it takes to get it or practice self-discipline. Nezzie chose the former. She decided not to take her meds. She chose to get in touch with you. She chose to party hard. You Simeon, are at fault as well. You didn't encourage Nezzie to take her medication because 'Medicated Nezzie' is boring and not the same Nezzie you grew to love. Am I wrong?"

After a long pause Simeon says, "No. But I love 'Crazy Nezzie.'"

"And look at the result. She's not healthy Sim, and neither are you. Misery loves company. She needs to get healthy and so do you. I've seen enough people on the streets to know that you're taking stuff. Long term Sim, it's gonna tear you apart. But I think you already know that."

For a moment Simeon stares at the TV instead of me. He's either angry or feeling convicted. "Damn sis," he says as he wipes his eye with his sleeve.

I say, "You're finally a full-timer at Sutton, a job you've waited for so long. Nezzie was a distraction, a way to get you off-track. You gave into her desires because it make you feel better about your addictions."

"But sis, before I saw Nezzie last month at the store, I had moved on from her. But now I think I'm in love with her. I want to help Nezzie stay on the right path."

"Sim, you can't help Nezzie if you don't help yourself first! And you can't really love her unless you really love Simeon Harrison."

He grins for the first time tonight. "You're right. Thanks Tracey. Man, I feel bad bringing my depressing ass to ruin your special night."

I grin as I hug him. "Boy please, you'll have to do a lot more to ruin my night. And by the way, what I just said is how Simon feels as well. But you wouldn't receive it the same way if he told you."

With a loud laugh he says, "That's for damn sure!"

"Can I get everyone's attention please?" Simon asks, an hour after dinner. "I know some of you have to leave, so I want to thank everyone for coming. Tracey didn't want anything big, which is hard for me when it comes to parties. So, if you're here tonight it's because you're special to my wife."

I smile as I stand next to my husband, asking God in my mind on what to share with everyone. I don't have to say anything except a "thank you" but this is a rare opportunity to have all my peoples in one setting.

"I wanted to celebrate her promotion because my wife is the toughest and bravest woman I know," he says before everyone applauds. Then Simon turns to me during a long pause, trying not to shed a tear. "Babe, with all the crime you deal with every day and the racism you put up with, then come home to deal with me and still be a loving mother to Symon and Symone, you are a real superhero. I thank God for you, and I love you."

My heart melts and I have to kiss my white chocolate and best friend on his sexy lips. Everyone applauds again.

"Love you too babes," I reply. "Thank you everyone for coming. The fact that you made time on a Saturday during your busy schedule to come tonight means the world to me. I love you all."

"LOVE YOU TOO TRACEY!" Audre shouts.

I laugh before taking a long pause. "I never expected to become a Detective Sergeant this soon in my career. The Lord really has been good to me. I was just going to show my gratitude and let y'all do your thing but... there is something that I want to share with you."

23

TRACEY

"For a long time, people young and old ask me 'What made you want to become a cop? What led you to deal with Special Victims' cases?' Usually I answer 'I have a passion for justice' or 'I'm a big fan of Olivia from Law and Order' but it goes deeper than that. For the first ten years of my life, I wanted to be a fashion designer believe it or not."

My guests laugh with me, some in disbelief. They have little idea of what I'm about to share.

I continue, "But that all changed on a hot summer day in Toronto..."

It was a hot and humid day. My mother took us to the water park in a suburban neighborhood, miles away from our home in the inner city. It was mid-week, so the park wasn't too packed which was great for us. More space to run around and do foolishness. My two siblings and I always looked forward to playing with water until we got too hungry or tired.

"Tracey, I'm gonna walk over to the snack bar to get you all some food," my mother told me. "Watch your brother and sister, I'll be back shortly."

"Ok Mom," I said, then ran back to the water.

We were busy splashing and playing tag in the pool when suddenly we hear some loud barking.

"AHHH! I don't wanna play anymore!" my sister, Sasha, screamed as she ran behind me. "I'm scared."

It was two White men and a woman, the men handling two huskies with leashes. They were walking in the wading pool, letting the dogs bark ferociously at us, scaring us out of the water.

"Those dogs aren't allowed in the water!" I screamed at the grown-ups with fear. I was reminded always to respect my elders, but they were breaking the rules.

The woman turned to me and said, "What did you say, nigger?"

That was the first time I heard that word other than hearing it in a movie or a grown-up conversation. Now I was petrified but I refused to back down.

"W-w-we just wanna swim," I said with my legs shaking.

"Ain't no niggers allowed to swim in this park!" As she said that, she pushed me down, causing me to hit my head on the concrete. "You and your nigger brother and sister pollute the water! If y'all were in Mississippi, they'd lynch your black asses!"

"TRACEY!" My mother rushed to my attention, noticing the blood on the back of my head. My siblings ran to her sobbing. "Oh my God! Rest on this towel. Bobby and Raquel, stay with your sister."

I saw my mother grab a can of mase out of her purse, confronted the evil lady and said, "Woman, you messed with the wrong child!"

"AHHHH! YOU CRAZY NIGGER!" she screamed in pain after getting sprayed in her eyes. Mom proceeded to kick her in the stomach and repeatedly punched her in the face.

"Nigger, you gonna die for hitting my wife!" one of the men said. "ATTACK BOY!"

He released the leash of his dog and it jumped on my mother.

"MOMMY!" I yelled in horror.

"My mother had to get her leg amputated. I suffered a concussion. My siblings and I were emotionally scarred for years. All because of the color of our skin. During my teenage years I was a very angry person. It didn't take much for me to lash my attitude on you. Just look at me the wrong way and I'll make you regret it.

I absolutely hated White people. If I seemed nice to them it was always fake. I wanted to go to an American Black college, but I didn't have enough tuition money, so I had to settle for a nearby university. Thus, I made the most of the opportunity right away- I joined the Black Students Association, Black Students Union, Students of Color, any student organization that allowed me to speak against White people. It was my early highlights of going to post-secondary school.

The thing that pissed me off the most was my dorm room. All the Black people in the dorm were getting black roommates except me. Olive Grant was White. Immediately I submitted a request for a Black roommate, but it wasn't going to happen because skin color was not a valid reason for a switch. I tried to find multiple reasons to dislike Olive for the first two weeks, but I couldn't. She kept her area clean, had proper hygiene, never played loud music, didn't force a conversation if I didn't want to talk. When Olive wanted a friend to visit the room, she gave me notice. We didn't hang out or have long conversations, but we had a good mutual respect for each other. And it was Olive who helped me change my life once again..."

It was almost five in the morning and I was still awake from studying. I was surprised that Olive was still out because she is all-study and no party. Her luggage was still in the dorm, so she didn't go home for the weekend.

As I got under my blanket ready to wind down, Olive entered the room. My side lamp was still on, so I was able to see her unusual appearance. Her hair was out of place and she looked quite dazed. As Olive took off her clothes and put on her bathrobe, I sat up and asked, "Hey Olive, are you feeling okay?"

Olive sat on her bed with a calm demeanor and said, "I think I was raped."

Not expecting that answer I asked, "What? Are you serious? Did you say 'no' or 'stop' while it was happening?"

"I-I think so. I don't know. I can barely remember, I don't know!" She started crying as she got up to grab a towel. "Maybe I'll feel better after a shower."

"NO!" I startled Olive because I've never snapped at her before. "I know you may feel nasty or disgusting but we have to report this to the police and you have to get a test."

"We?" she asked.

"Yes, I'll go with you."

When I said that, it hadn't occurred to me that I was offering to help a White woman. At that moment the one thing I disliked more than White people was injustice for women.

"You may change your mind after I tell you who did it."

Was it someone I knew?

"I won't change my mind," I promised.

"It was Trevor Brown."

I was shocked and angry; he's my boyfriend's best friend.

Later that day, Ryan ran up to me as I was walking to my evening class. We had been dating for a few months and he was the star wide receiver for the university football team. "Hey I've been calling your dorm all day," he said. "How's your roommate doing?"

"Not good," I answered. "Her parents came and picked her up after we came back from the police station."

"Tracey, that's what I gotta talk to you about. If or when this goes to court, and if Olive's lawyer asks you to testify, I need you to decline."

I stopped walking and stared at Ryan for a few seconds. "Say what?"

"Trevor is going to plead not guilty. But Olive is White and Trevor's Black, so we know already that his chances aren't good."

"Does Trevor believe that he raped Olive?" I asked quietly because we were in a public setting.

"He said no and that it was consensual."

"Do you believe Trevor raped Olive?"

A few seconds passed by before he said, "I don't know."

"Well boo, I will tell you what I believe. When Olive told me that Trevor raped her, I told her that I wanted full details of what she could remember and I want the truth. Olive believes that she was date raped and couldn't remember what she said. But she also had some vaginal wounds according to the rape test at the station. I believe Olive was raped, Ryan. Your boy made a horrible mistake and he needs to face the consequences."

"So, would you testify if you're asked to in court?"

"If she needs me to testify, yes I will."

Suddenly I saw a darker side of Ryan that I've never seen before. "Wow. I would've never thought you'd be a sellout."

Ryan said a trigger word that instantly made my blood boil.

"Negro, you better explain yourself before I embarrass the hell outta you!"

"Trace, how do you think it will look if you, a Pro-Black woman, fights against your own people to defend a White girl? And what about me? Trevor is the best QB right now in college and I'm his number one target. If he goes to jail-"

"Are you hearing the mess that's coming out of your mouth right now?" I asked out loud. "Did you really make this about you?"

"No Trace, but you don't understand-"

"Yes, I do understand! My roommate was R-A-P-E-D and you're more concerned that the boy who did it won't be able to throw you a damn football?

And lemme tell you this one time and you better not forget it: whatever happens in this case doesn't affect my blackness one damn bit! I will always fight for my people. But it doesn't matter if Trevor is Black, White, Green, whatever- if he's guilty of rape, he deserves a fair punishment. And Olive doesn't deserve what happened to her no matter what color she is."

"Tracey, you're gonna regret it if you do it."

"And you're gonna regret this conversation. Lose my number, we're done!"

"I ended up being a witness in court," I say. "Trevor was guilty and sent to prison. Rumors were spread about how I was a sellout and as a result, I lost the respect of some of my own people. But I didn't care. My roommate helped me to break down the hate I had for White people. I also knew that I wanted to help special victims. Sixteen years later, by the grace of God, I'm doing what I love to do and I'm still healthy and alive to do it well.

I will always be passionate about anti-racism and helping people. Becoming a Detective Sergeant will be a challenge, but I know that the Lord will never give me more than I can handle. I'm excited for what's in store for my family and every one of you that's here tonight. Thank you for coming. 2020 is going to be a great year! Amen?"

"Amen!" everybody says and cheers. There are smiles all around and some teary-eyed. I hug everyone who's in my home, and they each give me words of encouragement. It's truly a great evening and it feels good to finally share my past to family and friends.

24

AUDRE

March 7, 2020

"I'm telling you Audre, as soon as your 90-day probation is up, you need to sign up to attend a week at Port Huron." Kareem Chan says to me as sit at the table during lunch.

"Port Huron? Why, what goes on there?" I ask.

"The Education Centre for the Union is there, about three hours away from the plant. All wages and expenses paid, you go there and gain knowledge on becoming a better activist in your workplace and community."

"That sounds good. I can go away for a week and leave my boys, who are old enough to take care of themselves."

"That's good. You'll enjoy being away from all the everyday distractions of work and other stuff. I'll bring you an application if you're interested."

"Yes, please and thank you Kareem. It's so good to see you as a District Union Rep for the entire shift. Especially after all the racist crap you tolerated in high school."

Kareem sighs. "Thanks Dre. I still put up with it here being an Asian with an African-American name. But I have much thicker skin now. We need more workers of color in our committee and I hope to see you on it in the near future."

After finishing my lunch, I have a few minutes before the line starts so I proceed to the washroom. It's a late Saturday morning and I'm feeling anxious, and when this happens, I usually feel like throwing up. Nothing comes out when I face the toilet, but the feeling's not going away. It's the same feeling I had hours before Hank died. I want to go home but with the day shift already half over, I place my phone in my pocket and decide not to focus on the negative.

One hour later, we are sitting down again because the line isn't moving due to a shortage of parts. Now I'm really itching to go home, along with every other worker on the Door Line. I just want to spend some quality time with my boys. My plan is to take them out to Red Lobster and a movie. For the most part, the twins are staying out of trouble- as far as I know. Tracey offered to keep a tracker on Terrell but I turned it down. He and Tristan need to be able to trust their only parent.

Why do I still have a crappy feeling in my stomach?

As I walk to the vending machine to buy a ginger ale, my phone starts ringing. It's my little brother Will, who usually texts me as his first option. "Hey bro, what's up?"

"Dre, I'm at the hospital with the twins. I found Terrell in front of your crib unconscious and beaten up so I rushed him here."

Thank God it only took a fifteen-minute drive to arrive at the hospital. My heart is racing, tears are flowing and it's hard for me to stay calm because my intuitions were right once again. The moment I got off the phone with Will, I told my team leader what happened and he told me to just leave without waiting for the supervisor's approval.

"Excuse me, I need to see Terrell Wilson. I'm his mother," I say to the man at the reception desk.

Will approaches me and gives me a hug. "Will, what happened? Where's my baby?" I sob uncontrollably.

"Sis, he'll be alright. It looks like a concussion, bruises, and possibly a broken wrist."

"Da hell? Who da fa- who did this to Terrell? Where's Tristan?"

"Tristan is in the room with Terrell. I gotta give you a heads up before we go in there. I was coming over just to bring you some food from Mummy and Terrell is lying on the front yard. Sis, I believe he's pushing."

My blood starts to boil in the midst of my tears. "I had a feeling he was- damn! Why? Dammit, I wanna comfort him and kick his stupid ass at the same time! Did Tristan know?"

Will gives me a "c'mon" expression. "You know I don't need to answer that."

Tristan is walking towards us. My mind is going freaking crazy. I have so many questions, plus a mental battle is going on between Nurturing Mama and Kickass Mama. "Tristan, how long has your brother been dealing? And may I warn you that there are huge consequences if you lie in front of me and your uncle."

"Since January," he admits. "You haven't seen how much money he's been making because he's kept it in his locker at school. Last week someone broke in his locker and stole the money he owed his dealer. He didn't have it, and this beatdown was a final warning."

"And who the hell did this?"

"Mama, I don't know. Terrell tells me everything but he won't tell me who he works for."

I let out a loud sigh. "Why Terrell, why. Can I see him now?"

After the doctors did some X-rays, we are allowed to enter the room, but I tell Will and Tristan to wait outside for a few minutes. I have to see for myself if Terrell is willing to be open to me, without having a means to escape like he does at home. "Hey baby," I say without choking up. "How are you feeling?"

"Hey Mama," Terrell says, looking like he's embarrassed. "My wrist is broken and they say I have a concussion, but I'll be fine. I just wanna get the hell outta here."

"I'll talk to the doctor and see when you can be released. But I'm not in a rush for you to go home. You don't know how to stay home."

Terrell stays silent and gives me very little eye contact.

"Why are you always on the go Terrell? Are you pushing?" I ask quietly to avoid the suspicious ears in the room.

A tear falls from his eye. "I'm sorry Mama."

I caress my hand on his face. "Your father being gone has been tough on all of us. I haven't been able to provide financially like when we were both working. For that, I'm sorry. But baby, the game is not the answer. Do you want us to live life without you and Pops?"

Terrell shakes his head. "I'll quit. I promise."

"Damn right you will! How much do you owe?"

"Nine hundred," he says quietly.

More frustration builds. That's more than my entire weekly paycheck.

"Who's the guy that did this to you?"

I wait for a response as he closes his eyes.

"Terrell?"

His eyes squeeze tighter.

"Son, who the hell did this to you?"

A tear falls out of his closed eyes.

"Terrell!"

"I don't want you involved, Mama," he says after I startle him.

"It's too damn late for that. Who did this to you?"

"Don't make me have to tell you Mama."

Why is he so damn stubborn?

I calmly respond, "I won't make you respond Terrell, because just like your brother, you have your daddy's stubbornness all over you. But I'll tell you that if you won't answer my question and I find out who it is from someone else, expect big time consequences from me. So, I'll ask you one more time- Who. Did. This. To. You?"

I walk out of the room ten minutes later after speaking to the doctor about Terrell's condition. "Y'all can go back in," I say to Will and Tristan. "I'm going downstairs to buy us some lunch from the food court."

After Tristan tells me what he wants to eat he goes into the room. Will approaches me and asks if I'm okay.

"No. Terrell won't tell me who did this. His silence is his way of protecting me. But if he doesn't pay them back..."

I start crying but the tears are more of anger than fear.

Will says, "I'll see what I can do. Once I find out who did this, I'll let you know."

"Please Will. I'm not over losing Hank. I can't lose my son too."

Giving me a huge hug, I place my head on his shoulder. "I got you Dre. I got you."

"Dammit Hank! Why are you gone when I really need you to handle this?" I cry out loud as I walk down the hallway.

<u>25</u>

<u>SKITTLES</u>

Almost two months has passed since I became a Sutton employee and for the most part it's been going well. Every other work day, I'm learning a new job on the Engine Line, something that my supervisor is starting to appreciate. Maybe this six-foot-one, long-haired black mechanic really knows car parts better than the average person. Brad will never admit it, but at least he's less of an arrogant prick around me.

I keep getting side mechanic jobs as word continues to spread about my services. That, plus my consistent weekly paycheck has been resulting in some bills getting paid and increased savings. For this, I truly thank God for his provision.

Donna and I have become Friends With Benefits. I've never been one to have sex with someone that I'm not dating but it seems to be working. We only get together every other weekend because she's not ready for another relationship. I have never dated a White woman so I'm still in the experiment phase. Can I be comfortable dating a White woman after how that White cop humiliated me several weeks ago? Only time will tell.

It's the second half of the morning shift on Saturday and I'm working next to a young Black lady that I've never met. We actually both attend Faith Worship Tabernacle but we never noticed each other. She's also from Trinidad, so she knows a lot of my mother's family. We talked while working until the shift was over. However, Donna's job wasn't far away and I notice that she looks upset. We're supposed to get together tonight at her place so I hope we're still cool. Also, I talk to other women while working every so often and it never bothered her. We aren't dating anyway, just FWB.

The buzzer goes off and I go to the washroom before leaving the plant. Most of the time Donna and I walk out together to the parking lot. I come out of the washroom and she is gone. Donna usually tells me if she has to rush out after work. Maybe she is pissed off at me.

ME

Hey, I thought you were going to wait for me.

DONNA

Oh wow, you noticed I was gone?

Damn. She's upset.

ME

Are we still meeting up tonight?

DONNA

Sure whatever.

Actually don't bother. See you on Monday.

I roll my eyes and release a long sigh. Forget texting, I have to call her. "Hey. Are you ok? What's going on?"

"I'm fine," Donna says.

"Like hell you are. Why aren't we hanging out tonight?"

"I don't feel like hanging out anymore."

"Why? You were looking forward to it during lunch break."

"Well, I changed my mind, alright. Leave me alone."

"Not until you give me the reason why you're canceling on me. You're always one hundred with me Donna. Don't stop now."

I wait for a reply. Silence.

"Is it about me chatting with the student next to me today?"

No reply.

"Is it, Donna?"

No reply.

"Donna!"

"Yes, dammit, yes!"

I grin. "What's the big deal? We're only friends, right? Isn't that our agreement?"

"Yeah, but I can't do this anymore. I feel like crap. Too stressful."

I'm feeling confused. This is a side of Donna I'm not used to at all.

"What's too stressful? Us being friends?"

"Skittles, what the hell? Do I have to spell it out for you? It's either we go back to being friends without benefits, or we become something. Not in the middle."

I feel chills. Decision time is here sooner than I expected. Is this recently divorced mother of three the right woman for me? Is Donna the lady that God wants me to be with? I will have to find out from Him later because Donna is fun to be around, incredibly sexy, and just thinking about her is making me hot.

"Ok. Let's do it. I like you a lot, Donna. We enjoy hanging out together. You don't judge me at work based on my looks or appearance. And you already know I think you're fine as hell."

"Well Skid, I love our friendship and you make me laugh. You look tough but there's a sensitivity about you that I love. You go to church but you don't judge me for not being religious. I enjoyed being FWB but today, when you were talking with that girl all shift long, I was really feeling some kind of way. I really don't want to share your sexy ass with any other woman."

Donna admitting her wanting to possess me as her own gets me feeling harder.

I say, "You mention church. If we do become a couple, I want you to go to church with me."

"Every week?"

"If you can, but if you can't I won't stress about it. One week at a time."

"Ok. I can't promise but I'll do my best. Also, if we're gonna be together, I don't mind you talking to other women, but if you or any thot disrespects me, I will cut-"

"Hey hey hey, I got it. My lady gets all my love and respect."

"Good. Hey, when you come over bring some Skittles, ok?"

"Sure. What kind, sour or original?"

"Original. There's a game I want us to play, it's called 'Taste the Rainbow'."

"Ohh kay. Are you the rainbow?"

She laughs. "You'll find out when you get here. How soon can you come over?"

I get out of my car and open the trunk to grab some Skittles. "Thirty seconds. I'm in your driveway."

"What? You creepy-ass stalker!"

An hour later, I'm lying on Donna's chest under the sheets while she caresses my hair. My body is relaxed but my mind isn't at peace. Eyes are wide awake staring at the ceiling.

"You wanna order in tonight?" she asks. "Pizza, wine, Netflix and chill?"

"Sure," I say.

Looking at me, Donna asks, "You ok? You haven't said anything in the last fifteen minutes."

"There's something I need to share with you before we go forward in our relationship because you deserve my honesty."

"What is it? Don't make me nervous, Skittles. Are you bisexual?"

"What? No no, not at all. This has nothing to do with sexual preference. Different subject. Remember my first day of work, when I arrived late?"

"How could I forget? Damn I almost missed doing an engine when I first saw you."

"Well, I wasn't late because of tardiness. I was pulled over by the cops."

"For what, speeding?"

"For no reason expect DWB. Driving While Black."

She's not responding, but I don't expect her to.

"I was very early heading to work, just enjoying my music. This cop followed me for blocks and as soon as I select a track on my phone, which was hanging from the windshield, he pulled me over. Dude asked me tons of questions hoping to find a reason to arrest me. Made me come out of my car in the freezing cold just to search my vehicle, which was hella embarrassing as people drove by. They probably thought I was a criminal. Anyways, the man finished searching my Charger and tells me to wait in the car. Donna, he spent a freaking half hour in his police car doing who knows what, probably searching hard to find stuff on me but couldn't find nothing. End result, he tells me that I'm just receiving a warning. He then followed behind me until I pulled into Sutton, threatening to pull me over again if I go over the speed limit. That's what made me late to work."

"Oh my God," Donna says as she hugs me from behind. "I'm sorry you had to deal with that. Did you report him?"

"Not right away because I didn't get his badge number."

"How come you never told me about this earlier? Why now?"

"Because Donna, I tried to move on from it but what made it worse is that the cop who did this was your ex-husband's friend. Tucker Mayfield."

"WHAT? Tucker did that to you?"

I nod. "I don't forget many faces. When he gave me the same look at the restaurant that he gave me when I rolled down my window, I knew it was-"

"That mutha- no wonder him and Dylan get along so well! Unbelievable!"

"Donna, I mention this because now that we're together, expect your ex to give us a hard time. If Tucker thought I was a criminal that day, I can't imagine the lies he told Dylan about me."

"What can Tucker tell Dylan about you? Do you have a criminal record?"

"No I don't, but if Tucker has a problem with Black people, he will convince Dylan that I'm a problem. Just giving you a heads up. Anything they possibly tell you about me will be pure lies."

"Baby, I know who you are and I don't give a damn what Dylan thinks about you, because it's about how I think about you. As for Tucker, I already cancelled him months ago. Now after this, I don't want his racist ass anywhere near my kids. You already know I'm a grown-ass woman who can take care of my own damn self. If we want to be together, that's all that matters right?"

"That's it," I answer.

Donna is a woman that makes me feel good as a man. I love that confidence that she carries, and she's fearless. But now that I'm her BF, I'm not sure if it's worth it if I have to deal with her ex-husband.

26

JESSICA

The day is finally here. My ninetieth working day at Sutton. Everyone here says that once I hit day ninety, I'm officially off probation. This means that I'm fully represented by the Union if there are any problems between myself and management. This is a huge monkey off my back and I'm so looking forward to being an official employee.

That being said, it doesn't mean that I enjoy my job. I'm still on the same job that requires me to use the right side of my body and the pain is stronger than ever. I still have to take muscle relaxers and Tylenol 3 at least twice a week. A couple of days were so bad that I had to call-in sick, which is frowned upon when you're on probation but I had to put my self-care first. One of my absentee days was on a holiday that we were scheduled to work. The day after was the first time I ever saw my always-smiling supervisor look upset.

The main thing that should matter the most is that this forty-something Black woman is a hard worker and I give my one-hundred even when it hurts like hell. I can only give the credit to the Lord because if it wasn't for Him, I probably would've already quit. But I'm here, day nine-zero. I'm trying not to get excited because I still gotta finish the shift.

My team leader has these small forms available to book a day off on the weekend. I'm going to grab a few because I'm going to need a Friday or Saturday off for rejuvenating and to spend time with the kids. It's going to feel amazing. What's also amazing is God's provision over our finances. Darian and I are on a good pace towards becoming debt-free. I hate working through pain but it's worth it when bills are getting paid without any major struggles.

Only thirty minutes away from the final buzzer. Darian is bringing the van and I'm going to drive it home. I don't think he made dinner, so I'm just going to order pizza and relax. Shoot, I think I deserve it. The probation storm is almost over.

Feeling a pat on my shoulder, I look to my left and see Moe, my team leader.

"Hey Jessica, the Union Rep needs to see you."

DARIAN

As usual, I'm scrambling around the house trying to get my stuff together for work. It seems like whenever I'm on the afternoon shift, I tend to wait until the last minute to pack my lunch, notebook for writing my novel, BT earbuds, phone charger, wallet and keys. This is after wrapping up homeschool and preparing lunch for the kids. Homeschool was light today, but I didn't care because I'm too excited about Jessica ending her probation.

For three months, I was very concerned about Jessica's health since the accident and how it's affecting her at work. Mentally and physically, she's been tough as nails. Friday was her 89th working day, and if management wanted to fire her it would have been then or earlier. It didn't happen. God is so good. As a result, I had a peace of mind over the weekend. We are on our way towards our goal of financial freedom.

I should have been at the Sutton plant for 2:30pm but I haven't even left my driveway. Procrastination has really kicked my ass today. My youngest daughter Janiya, who is only two has been really clingy so I decide to take her with me. It's almost 3:00pm when I leave the house, absolutely unacceptable. Now I have to drive like a mad man just to get to my shift on time.

I look back at Janiya who is wide awake, as if she's anticipating something. "Hey boo-boo, you ok? We're gonna pick up Mommy now!"

It's not safe to drive and text, but I forgot to update Jessica on my ETA.

ME

Hey babes, I'm so sorry to have you waiting. I'll be there in less than 10 minutes.

Surprisingly, she doesn't respond right away. Five minutes later, Jessica sends a reply that shocks the hell out of me.

JESSICA

Hey hun, np.
I'm in a meeting with management. I'm about to get fired.

JESSICA

There is a cart waiting for me and on it is my Union Rep Jeff Conroy and Steve Bateman, who I believe is a District Rep but I've never met before now. Not much is said as we drive towards the HR office, but it's not like I need an explanation. I just need God's favor for what I think is going to happen.

We enter the room and waiting for me is Chad, my supervisor. There's also a lady from HR who doesn't introduce herself but I didn't care to know. I take a seat, ready to hear what they have to say so I can go home.

"Jessica, you are here for your 90-day evaluation and our decision as to whether or not you should continue as an employee of Sutton Assembly," Chad begins. "During your probation period you have taken multiple days off and also you have not performed your job according to the company's standards."

Say what?

"Underperformed? Can you explain please, I don't understand," I say.

Chad tries to explain about the one day I was putting on a particular car part the wrong way and I did it multiple times. I remember that day. Yes, I made a mistake with the assembling of the part but I eventually corrected it and never repeated the mistake again. Then, Chad explains another incident which was very minor and insignificant in my opinion.

"I can understand being let go because of my absences, which were legitimate because I wasn't well," I explain, "but one thing I was told during the orientation prior to working was that if I don't perform my job well, then management will put me somewhere else. You kept me on the same job for the entire probation, so obviously the best that I could, otherwise you would've moved me a long time ago!"

"Jessica, everything I mentioned is all documented in this file. I know that I wasn't your supervisor when you started, but I'll bring in Bobby and Kevin to verify the evaluation."

A few minutes later, my first supervisor Bobby Golic and my current alternate supervisor Kevin Sabuto come into the office. Suddenly, this Black woman is surrounded by three supervisors, one HR lady and two union reps, all White. I don't expect this to go well, but I'm not leaving without proving that I'm a valuable employee.

Bobby and Kevin echo the issues that Chad explained earlier. The trio are on one accord in regards to downplaying my performance. They are the lying Three Stooges. I do the same job for three months and I didn't perform it well? That's like drinking filtered water for three months, the body maintains good health, but you tell everyone that the water is polluted. Are they really intimidated by me because I'm a

Black woman? Kevin is talking but I don't care what he has to say as because he's only been my supervisor for a few days and I gave him zero issues. But when Bobby speaks, I can't stay silent.

"From your first week you asked me if you can go to the medical office," Bobby says. "Seems to me you're working just to collect WSIB."

"WSIB? What's that?" I ask, not knowing it means Workplace Safety and Insurance Board, money that workers collect if they can't work due to injury from the workplace. "I was in pain because of my accident one month before getting hired. When I completed the job interview process, I actually failed the physical. I had to get an approval from my family doctor and then re-take the physical a second time to get the green light from Sutton. However, despite all that you guys still decided to place me on a job that requires me to use the right side of my body for long periods of time. I was hit by a truck on the right side of my body! So excuse me if I had to see medical on my second day of work due to the excruciating pain I was dealing with! And Bobby, I heard you speaking on the phone with the nurse while I was in the medical office. You tried to make her think that I was a liar! How would you know if I was lying when you barely knew me other than the fact that my husband used to work for you?"

Bobby asks, "If you are telling the truth, why do you go by two different names?"

"What are you talking about?"

"We call you Jessica but your first name is Charlene."

If he really using this to downplay my character?

"Bobby, that is correct. Charlene is my first name but I'm known by my middle name Jessica. I'm not trying to hide anything. If you call me Charlene or Jessica, I'll still answer. It doesn't mean that I'm a liar. Nothing that I did while working here was dishonest. If you let me go because of my absences, so be it. But I did that job for the entire probation period which means one thing; I did my job well. My team leader said more than once that I was doing well. Someone from management, who's not in this room said the same thing. Also, whatever decision you decide to make, I will leave this room knowing that I did the job well."

After I leave the room with the two Union guys, Steve says, "You did an admirable job in there. You defended yourself very well."

Did I hear somebody from the Union speak to me just now? I thought this District Rep and my Union Rep had their tongues removed because they said nothing during the meeting. Nothing! Not a single word. I thought that we would have a pre-meeting to plan on what would be discussed. Didn't they want to know my side of the story before the meeting so they could properly defend me? Obviously not. They allowed the supervisors to have their way with HR, and if I was timid they would've destroyed my character. They really left a bad taste in my mouth about unions. If I was their skin color, would they have defended me better?

"Thanks," I reply just to be polite.

I went from a half hour away from becoming a full-time employee to being terminated in the span of an hour. I'm going home to be with my kids without returning to the plant tomorrow. I don't understand why God allowed this to happen, but today ends my chapter with Sutton.

DARIAN

ME

Nooooo! Praying right now!

"Father God, I need you to come through right now in Jesus' name!" I shout while driving. "Jessica doesn't deserve this! Change their decision, Lord! Give her favor!"

Now I'm late for work and nervous. I thought management didn't let anyone go in the 90th day. Why is this happening? Is it because of the missed days? It can't be because of her performance. My wife didn't work her ass off to be released because of a few sick days. Am I really going to have to work through today's shift knowing that my employer fired my wife?

To avoid losing my mind, I have to switch back to a faith mindset and believe that God will work a miracle.

Almost two minutes from arrival, Jessica texts me back.

JESSICA
That's it. I have been fired. (laugh emoji)
ME
No...

I want to yell in anger but I don't want to scare Janiya. If I could cry right now in frustration I would, but my eyes won't allow it. For a brief moment I can understand why a person would go postal because I'm so angry right now and I don't know how to deal with it. Prayer isn't working fast enough.

I park in the Kiss and Ride section with only three minutes away from start time. Janiya is falling asleep so I don't bother to wake her up with a goodbye. Jessica is waiting on the sidewalk, and all I want to do is comfort her for the rest of the day.

Staring at her big beautiful eyes, all I see are tears falling down Jessica's cheeks. I give her the best hug I can do in a short period of time.

"They lied so much, Darian," she sobs. "All they did in that meeting was lie."

"Babe, I'm so sorry. You don't deserve this. They did you wrong."

I can't believe I have to rush into work to build cars for this prick company. My skin is getting warm because I'm so pissed off. "Just go home and relax hun. I'm going to get to the bottom of this. Love you."

"Love you too."

Honestly, I don't have a plan but the first thing I want to do is talk to the Union as soon as possible, to find out if Sutton can get away with this termination. I'm speed walking the main aisleway because the one-minute warning buzzer goes off. Walking the opposite direction is my former supervisor, Bobby Golic. I clench my left fist.

The moment Bobby looks at me I swing my arm and punch him in the jaw.

"I TRUSTED YOU BOBBY! WHAT THE HELL WERE YOU THINKING, FIRING MY WIFE?"

That's the action that I want to do, but I know better. Not trying to have both spouses out of work.

Bobby pretends to not recognize me walking past him. I hate conflict but I'm ready to bring the noise.

"BOBBY, WHAT THE HELL? WHY DID YOU FIRE MY WIFE?"

Surprised that I yelled at him, he says, "Darian, she had it coming. She missed more than a few days of work."

"THAT'S BECAUSE SHE WAS IN AN ACCIDENT BEFORE GETTING HIRED! YOU KNEW THAT!"

"Darian-"

"EVERY TIME SHE CAME TO WORK, SHE WORKED HARD! YOU WERE WRONG, MAN! THAT WAS WRONG!"

Bobby had more to say, but the buzzer goes off and I'm running to my job, which I now regret. He deserves to be exposed in public for what he did to Jessica in private. I want to turn back and confront him again but it's too late.

"DAMMIT!" I threw my backpack at the computer by my workstation. My team leader, Gil, is doing my job and was surprised from my outburst.

"You ok buddy?" he asks.

"No Gil, I'm mad as hell right now! Sutton just fired my wife minutes ago! I need to talk to the Union now!"

"Oh, I'm so sorry buddy. They're pricks man. No problem, I'll tell them to come now."

"Thanks Gil."

As I wait for my Union Rep to show up, it hurts my mind to wonder why God allowed this termination to happen.

27

SIMON

It's Wednesday morning, the last day of work before my three-week vacation. I'm very excited but still stressed today because I have a list of things to do before Tracey and I leave on Friday to Dubai. Because the virus story won't go away, we decided last week that we aren't taking the twins with us on the cruise. Instead, they will stay with Tracey's relatives a couple of hours away from us. It's going to be some amazing quality time together, something that we need more than we can imagine.

During my breaks and lunch, I'm going to try and see my brother, Audre and Skittles. But first I see my boy Kareem walking down the main aisleway. Good timing because I'm pissed about what happened to Jessica.

"How was your trip?" I ask. "You just came back and I'm starting mine tomorrow."

"New York was nice bro," Kareem says. "It was only three days but it was a good getaway from here. I got your text yesterday about Jessica."

"Yeah, you go away and crap hits the fan. Darian calls me yesterday and he's furious. Three supervisors ganged up on Jessica and lied about her performance to get her fired. And you know what your alternate District Rep Steve Bateman and Jeff Conroy did in the meeting? Nothing Kareem! Left her to drown without a lifejacket!"

"God, help me. And this is one of the reasons why I fought for this position. To see workers of color get treated fairly, without prejudice or discrimination. And the second I go away from the plant-"

"White privilege takes over. And this is a white man saying that. My stepmom, my wife, Jessica- the stuff a Black woman has to do to succeed in North America. Makes me ashamed to be White sometimes. Of all the years I've worked with Darian, I've never known him to be this upset. Sutton did Jessica wrong man."

"I'm gonna look into it. She deserves to keep her job. If I was in that HR office, I would've fought my ass off for her- whether she's Black, White, Asian, whoever. That's what a union is supposed to do; fight systemic racism and not join forces with it."

I see Simeon looking at us from thirty-feet away so it's time for me to end the conversation. "For real. Yo, let's catch up when I get back."

"For sure," Kareem waves as I walk away. "Have a great trip, stay safe."

Simeon says after I approach him, "Bro that's crazy how the company did Jessica! I hope she fights that."

"How the hell did you- damn I forgot you can read lips," I say while shaking my head. When Simeon was a teenager, his best friend was hearing impaired, mischievous, and great at reading lips. Because my brother wanted to join him in causing trouble, he spent two years learning the craft. Also, since Simeon isn't deaf, no one knows he has this gift unless he tells them. "Yeah, it was a wrongful dismissal. I hope Kareem makes some noise about it in the union office."

"Boy, I better get past my ninety days with no issues. Bro, thank you so much for letting me use your truck while you're away. So, you'll bring the ride after work?"

"Yeah, but listen to me Sim. Trace and I trust that you will stay out of trouble and give it back the same way you got it. If I hear one word about you driving under the influence, we're done."

"I promise Simon. Ending my thing with Nezzie was a wake-up call. I only smoke weed now, no more of the other stuff. I wanna live a long life, brother."

"Just take things one day at a time. I'll see you at the crib later tonight."

I drive my cart to the Engine Line to visit Skittles, who is already working. Donna is working across from him so I wave to her.

"So, what's it like to work with your GF?" I ask Skittles.

"It's cool, y'know," he says. "Donna and I have a lot of fun together. We just really enjoy each other's company."

"It was good to see her at church on Sunday."

"Yeah, and she liked it. Donna was not used to it, but she loved how friendly the people were to her. It's a work in progress."

"Always. Happy for ya, bro. Hey, did you hear about Jessica?"

Skittles sucks his teeth. "Damn right I heard, Darian told me yesterday. That's messed up bro. Now I'm worried about passing probation, cuz even though I do impeccable work, my supervisor doesn't like me very much. I'm probably on the hot seat as well."

"Just pray for God's favor. Work hard and pray."

"Easier said than done, Simon. I love God, but how did praying for favor work for Jessica? Her faith level is way bigger than mine."

Skittles threw a question that I can't answer as a new believer. And it's a good one. Something I'll have to ask Pastor Marvin when I get to Dubai.

"Everything happens for a reason," I answer. "Something will work out for her. We serve the same God."

"I hope so. Hey, have you seen or heard from Dre lately?"

"Funny I was just about to ask you the same thing. She hasn't responded to any of my texts. Hopefully I'll have time to see her before the end of the shift. I'm leaving for Dubai on Friday morning."

"Bro, I envy you guys. Wish I was going on the cruise with y'all. Donna was saying the same thing when Pastor mentioned it at church. Looks fun."

"I just hope it happens. The news story about the cruise ship stranded at sea because of the virus has the trip in jeopardy."

"Damn."

"But we're leaving this country regardless," I say as I give him a fist pump. "Peace out."

28

AUDRE

"How's your son doing, Audre?" Margaret asks as we sit at the table during the ridiculously short ten-minute break.

"Terrell is slowly recovering," I explain. "Pretty bruised up, has a broken wrist. His concussion was mild so he's just having the occasional headache now."

"Looks like he has an early March Break from school."

"Yeah, wonderful. Twins are running up my utility and grocery bills already."

"Well, I hope he gets better soon. Be glad it's not worse, like that virus in China and Italy right now."

"Yeah, I know. That's some crazy mess going on. I heard hundreds are dying in Italy every day from it."

"It's insane. I hope that doesn't come to North America and if it does, we gotta kill it quick."

"That virus needs to stay across the ocean," I laugh before I see that Will is calling me. "Good morning brother."

"Hey. How's Terrell?" Will asks.

"Doing better. Still hasn't told me a damn thing about who beat him up. Please tell me you got something."

"Well, I do now. Don't ask what I had to do to get this info, it was tough."

Will knows a lot of people in our neighborhood and he works for a company that provides cell phones and home internet. I can only assume that he had to offer a free service or two just for someone to snitch.

"I won't ask," I say while walking away from the table. Margaret is watching with much curiosity.

"Ok. So, I heard the reason Terrell isn't telling you anything because while he was getting his beatdown, he promised to do a delivery to cover the debt. That's why he won't take your money. He's still in the game."

Hearing this was a stab to my heart. "Dammit Terrell. Why is he stressing me out like this? Who is this mutha who's giving me hell? You got a name?"

"Yeah, he goes by the name Blizzard. White boy, early twenties, slim yet muscular, short black hair. I just sent you a photo."

I look at my phone and view the photo in my WhatsApp. Gasping in shock, I zoom in the face to make sure I'm seeing it properly.

"Looking at him now. This guy hurt Terrell?"

"Yep, and get this: apparently he works at Sutton Motors. I don't know if he's in your area or even on the same shift as you, but that's where he works."

As Will is talking, I'm viewing the Door Line. About ten workstations away from me is the kid named Blizzard. That's why I gasped when I saw the photo. I worked with him just a few weeks ago.

"So, he's in my vicinity. This just got really interesting now."

"Dre, please don't put this in your own hands. Let's come up with a plan first and then take action. I'll come over after work."

"Ok," I say. "Thank you so much bro, you did amazing. Love you."

"Love you too."

The one-minute warning buzzer goes off. I look at the photo and the kid again. "Wow Chris, really? I thought you were a good guy."

It was three weeks ago when my supervisor placed me on a different job for a few days. It was a good job but the training for it took an entire shift to learn with ease. The person who taught me the job was Blizzard, who we all know as Chris. He was probably the nicest student worker on the Door Line- polite and patient. Chris didn't say much but he was a good teacher and good company. He smiles often and dresses like a computer geek. This young man assaulted my son?

Why can't this dealer be an ugly ass brother who's rude and disrespectful? Someone like this will be easy to be violent with. That is what I was hoping, but now I'm thinking that I should let Will kick his ass. But I want this done and over with.

I need a plan and I have until the end of the shift to think of a good one. Time to play a mix of Eminem, Wu-Tang, Mobb Deep and Public Enemy to tune everyone out. I think about my wounded son and how fortunate he is not to be dead. I think about how I vowed from the day the twins were born that I'll do anything to protect them from evil people. I think about a privileged White boy having his way by attacking my son, a Black teenager.

Nobody does harm to my children and gets away with it. Nobody.

SKITTLES

Dre, haven't heard from you in a minute. U good?

SIMON

Hey, I hope to catch you at work before the shift is done.

I ignore both messages. I haven't spoken to Simon, Tracey or Skittles since Terrell got attacked because I don't want their input or them getting involved. I have to complete this payback on my own, as the only parent of Terrell and Tristan Wilson.

I follow Chris and a couple of his friends out of the gate after the dismissal buzzer at 2:30pm. He doesn't notice me because there's a small crowd of people behind him. Chris starts walking left after he exits the pedestrian bridge. I have to go right because I'm parked in the opposite direction, so I speed walk to my minivan and drive to where he's parked. Thankfully, Chris is outside of his Sutton truck having a smoke with a couple of girls. I drive my van in front of his truck and place it in park, leaving the engine running. They stare at me, surprised and confused as to why an older Black woman is confronting them.

"Hey Audre, how are you?" Chris says with a big smile.

"Hi Chris. I want to give you something from someone who knows you. Do you know Terrell Wilson?"

His face shows the expression of "my friends don't know I'm a dealer."

"I don't know who you're talking about," Chris answers.

Liar.

I kick him so hard in the nuts his lady friends jump in fear.

"Do you remember now, Blizzard?"

"DAMMIT! WHAT THE HELL!" Chris yells, trying to create a scene.

"Do your nuts hurt? Betcha not as much as you hurt my son!"

I kick him a second time and Chris yells in agony. Because he doesn't want anyone in the parking lot to know of his true colors, he doesn't fight back. I open his pants and stuff the nine hundred dollars down his crotch. "Here, let me soothe those balls for you."

At this point, Chris' friends don't know whether to help, cuss me out or laugh. I didn't see if anyone is recording this on their phone, which I forgot to consider.

Chris moans and calls me the B-word before I place my hands on his neck and squeeze.

"I don't care what the hell you call me!" I say. "Just keep your sorry ass away from my son, now that you got your money. DO YOU UNDERSTAND ME BLIZZARD?"

Chris doesn't try to speak, nod or fight me while I'm choking him. No reaction makes me look like an angry Black woman torturing a young innocent White man. That's why I release my grip and quickly drive away.

My emotions are mixed. I feel better because I showed Terrell's attacker that he messed with the wrong woman. But now it hits me that my choice to take matters in my own hands may come back to bite me hard.

29

AUDRE

So many things can change in a week. Since confronting Blizzard, life at home hasn't been much easier. I never told the twins that I paid Terrell's debt, so the paranoia that they don't know anything is stressing them out. Maybe it's the fact that their Uncle Will has been at the house more often than not, and there's a baseball bat and mace in both the apartment and the minivan. Or maybe, it's because we eat corn beef and rice for dinner every night because I don't have grocery money.

Will is pissed at me for taking action on Blizzard without his assistance. Now, he's worried that something bad will happen to myself or Terrell, which is why he's frequently around. I feel like I did what I had to do as a mother and I won't apologize for that. Should I have done things differently? Only time will tell. I do regret not speaking to my friends while I was in revenge mode. Simon and Tracey are in Dubai and I didn't connect with them before they left. That's why I didn't know, until just a couple of days ago that Jessica got fired, Kareem told me.

Jessica and I have only been friends for a short time, but what I know about her is that she's a woman of God; a hard worker, a loving wife and mother. Sutton fired her. Like Jessica, I'm a Black woman and what this company did to her, they may also do to me. With a history of stopping the assembly and assaulting a student worker in the parking lot, my record has to be perfect from now until my ninety days are up, whenever that will be now that Covid is in North America.

The twins are home for an extended March Break because of the uncertainty of this virus. Outbreaks are happening throughout the city, yet we are still working. Sutton workers are worried and frustrated, so they are making noise to the Union that we need to close the plant to be safe and home with our families. Easy for them to say because they can collect employment insurance. As much as I'd love to be home right now, I don't know if I qualify to receive that based on lack of working hours. That's what I'm discussing with Skittles during our lunch break.

"We're about to get some breaking news soon," Skittles says. "Folks are scared right now, worried that they're gonna die if they catch the Rona. My parents don't want to close their convenience store because they need the money, but they don't want to get sick from a customer. However, their store is an essential business. If we stop working, I'm going to supervise the store so they can stay safe at home."

I say, "You're a good son Skittles. Me personally, I do hope we close for a short period, even though I'm broke AF right now. We gotta get our ninety days, Skittles. People who I don't even know heard about what I did to that boy in the parking lot and are calling me 'Mama Badass.' I know that some are thinking of me as an angry Black woman who beat up a young White man for no big reason at all, as if I have mental health issues. Nobody knows that he's a drug dealer."

"You'd think instead of judging you, they would judge the kid. Did anyone question why he hasn't been at work since the incident and why he took your money?"

I slam my hand on the table in agreement. "Thank you! I could say more on this but not here. Folks are watching us get loud. But getting back to this pandemic thing, if we shut down soon, I hope that me shutting down the line and attacking Chris will be a distant memory after we return to work. Hopefully. Because what they did to Jessica-"

"It's still pissing me off. I'm praying that Jess gets her job back with no seniority lost. And I believe and pray we'll complete our probation with no complications."

As Skittles says this, he places his big strong hands over mine and smiles. Suddenly, I feel a warm presence of comfort surround me. I'm looking at my childhood friend with a sense of attraction that I've never felt towards him before. If only he could kiss me right now...

"We got this," he says after he releases his hands from mine. His girlfriend comes to the table with their lunches from the cafeteria. That loving feeling is gone quicker than it came.

"Hey are you Au-dree?" she says with a warm smile.

"Au-dray, like Dr. Dre," I say extending my hand.

"Audre, my bad. I'm Donna, nice to meet you. Skittles talks about you and Simon all the time."

"Oh, does he?" I say while looking at Skittles who's already eating his curly fries. "Yeah, we've all been friends for almost thirty years, and now we all work at Sutton. Inseparable."

"Yeah, no kidding. How do you like it here?"

"Haha, can't say I love it but it pays well and provides for my family."

"Yep, that's what I hear from almost everybody from the last fifteen years."

While we're talking, I can't say that I dislike Donna. As long as she and Skittles have a genuine love and respect for each other, she's cool with me. I will be watching how Donna treats my boy as they continue dating.

The five-minute warning buzzer goes off. Time to walk back to my workstation.

"Alright, time to go," I sigh. "Nice meeting you Donna. Later Skid."

"Bye Dre," Skittles says. "I'll text you later."

"Nice meeting you too," Donna says. "Hopefully, we'll get news of going home early."

"Hope so," I smile.

Chris came to work for the last four hours of the shift. "Hi Audre," he says with a smile as he walks past me. I'm thrown off from his greeting, but it's an obvious front to make people think he's not a dealer and I'm a psycho. I look at Chris for two seconds then pretend he's not here.

While working, the conversations are all about the virus. There's a rumor floating that someone went home today because they were in close contact with a virus carrier. Everyone hopes that Sutton is the next business to close. "Send us home" is what a few are chanting. So I decide to tune out every noise by listening to an R & B mix on my Spotify.

Eight songs later, I take out an earbud because I hear cheers.

Margaret says, "Audre, I think we're done!"

"For real?" I ask. "Damn I hope you're right!"

Two minutes later the door line stops.

"That's it!" Trent shouts. "It's 11:24am, swipe out at 11:36am. Because of the pandemic, the plant will be closed until further notice. Take care everyone, and stay safe."

I quickly gather my belongings as I see my fellow workers head for the exit. If this is a lengthy shutdown, hopefully I can get employment insurance and spend quality time with my boys. Then, when the plant reopens, I will complete my probation and move forward with Sutton.

"Take care Audre," Margaret says. "Let's connect on Facebook and stay in touch."

"I don't do Facebook much," I admit, "but you gave me your number. I'll connect through WhatsApp. Stay safe, hun."

"You too. Hey Kareem, see you later."

Kareem arrives with the golf cart and waves. "Take care Margaret. Stay safe. Hey Audre."

"Kareem," I say. "This was a nice surprise. How long do you think the plant's going to stay closed?"

The expression on his face isn't joyful. Something is wrong. "No idea. I'm here to pick you up. We're going to HR."

A chill of fear rushes through my body. "Right now?"

He nods. "I'm ready to fight. Sutton's not getting away with this. Tell me everything that went down with Chris while we drive to the office."

I explain the story in full detail with Kareem as he slowly takes us there.

"Ok," he says after I'm done. "I gotta commend you for what you did. Your son is very lucky to have you as a mother. I'm gonna tell you what was reported to me. One of the ladies who was with Chris is the niece of Vito Martino."

I gasp. "The Plant Manager?"

"Yes. She told him that you attacked her boyfriend and accused him of a crime he didn't commit. And because of Vito's conversation with you, when you stopped the line in January, he's not willing to give you a third chance. But this meeting is when we can plead your case and-"

"Wait wait wait! This is some-"

I stop myself from going off on Kareem because he's not the one trying to fire me.

"I'll save what I have to say in the meeting. Kareem, we've been friends for years, but I'm asking you as a District Representative. Defend me like your salary depends on it!"

In the meeting room is Trent, a lady from HR, my Union rep Johnny, Kareem and myself.

"Audre," Trent begins, "I want to start by saying that you are not here because of your work performance. You have performed very well on every job you know on the Door Line. You arrive to work on time and haven't missed a single day. If I could have every person on the Door Line with your work ethic, I'd be a very happy supervisor.

This is about the incident that occurred in the parking lot at the end of the shift on March 11th. You assaulted and threatened Chris Silverman, thus making him unable to return to work for five days after, due to injury and fear for his safety."

As he's talking, I shake my head.

"You were given another chance after refusing to comply with management after stopping the Door Line during the month of January. The downtime cost the company thousands of dollars in lost time. We were going to wait until the end of your probation period to make a move, but because of the sudden closure of the plant due to the pandemic, our re-opening is unknown. When this happens, you will not be returning to Sutton Motors."

I take a deep breath because I don't want to cry. Terminated? I have three mouths to feed and bills up my ass, so Trent is about to hear a mouthful.

"Wow, okay this is a lot to swallow, but I won't do it because I refuse to swallow crap. Let me start with 'the assault.' Chris Silverman is not the kind young man that everyone in this plant thinks he is. Outside this assembly plant, Chris Silverman is a drug dealer known as Blizzard. My son who's in high school foolishly agreed to work for him and owed Chris money. When it wasn't paid on time, Chris assaulted my son, giving him a concussion and breaking his wrist. Do you have kids, Trent?"

"Uh, no I don't."

"Okay, are you married?"

"Yes I am."

"Ok, so what if someone brutally attacked your wife and-"

"Husband."

"Oh. Okay, so what if someone brutally attacked your husband and that person was at your workplace?"

"My husband is a 280-pound bodybuilder, so whoever beats him up would have to be a monster."

This isn't going well.

"What I'm trying to say is that as a mother, I will do whatever it takes to protect my children. I simply gave Chris the money my son owed him after kicking his balls, choking his neck and telling him to leave my son alone. I did not threaten him."

"His girlfriend said you threatened him."

"Well, this is my side of the damn story!" I snap. "I had no need to threaten him because he got the damn point! As for Chris not coming to work for injury, I get it because I kicked the crap out of his little nuts, but not coming to work because he fears me? That's absolutely ridiculous. Chris is fooling everyone in this plant.

Let's go back to the time I stopped the line. Your student worker, Carolyn, had a seizure and injured her head. We thought she was in critical condition. You pulled her away from the line and expect us to continue working as if nothing happened! Where's the compassion? Someone's life is more important than a few damn vehicles!"

"I was following orders to start the line, Audre. Our head office in Detroit only cares about the numbers and the bottom line."

"Well, I was following my heart. It felt like it was the right thing to do."

Kareem says, "Allow me to step in, Audre. Trent, this is an unfair termination and I'm going to tell you why. When Audre stopped the line, she acted on the need to help another sister in an emergency. Her physical confrontation with Chris was a mother seeking payback for what he did to her son. In both cases, Audre acted because of her compassion for someone in need. That shows you the kind of woman she is, not the psycho woman that Chris and his girlfriend are telling others in the plant.

Next, this incident was in the parking lot. Although it's still the property of Sutton, the incident did not affect the production of cars. There was no damage to the company property. A lot of crazy things happens in the parking lots every day that is known but not reported, yet nothing is done about it.

Finally, I'm going to recall another incident that took place during the lunch hour on January 14th of this year. Fredrick Martin was choking the life out of Jamie Nguyen in the lunch area, your Door Line area as a matter of fact."

I say, "It was right next to where I was sitting. That happened on my second day of work."

"Right," Kareem continues. "Fredrick also threatened Jamie. Audre didn't threaten Chris. Fredrick only got a two-day suspension and returned to work like nothing happened."

Trent says, "Kareem, even if Audre only gets a suspension, it will still result in a termination once her ninety days are up."

"Then give her the suspension on her 91st day!"

"I can't do that."

"Why not? What Sutton is doing is a racist move!"

"How so?"

"Fredrick is White and only received a two-day suspension. Audre is a Black woman who did less and you're calling for a termination! Sounds like White Privilege to me!"

I want to smile but I stay serious. Kareem is preaching up in here.

The HR lady enters the conversation. "Kareem, in the Sutton Motors workplace manual it states that if there's any forms of violence on the company property it can lead to a suspension or a dismissal. And because Audre is still on probation, the company has the choice to go straight to a dismissal without the Union's approval."

"I understand that," says Kareem, "but ethically it's wrong. You will be firing a Black widow of two children because she tried to protect her son from a criminal."

"Allegedly," Trent says.

"HE'S A DAMN CRIMINAL!" I shout. "After all that was said, you still think that prick is a saint?"

I can't hold back the tears anymore. My guard is down but I refuse to leave this room without making them feel guilty as hell for even thinking of firing me.

Kareem hands me a tissue. "You guys know what's the right thing to do here. Audre is a damn good worker, you said it yourself Trent. She deserves to be a Sutton employee."

Johnny, who has been silent the entire meeting says, "I second that. Letting Audre go would be a huge mistake. She's a passionate person that also puts passion in building a great Sutton vehicle."

I walk out with my Union Reps ten minutes later. Johnny waves goodbye to us as Kareem drives me to the exit. At this point, I don't know how to react about what took place.

"I'm sorry Audre. I really feel like I let you down in there," Kareem says.

"Don't be," I say. "You represented me well. Sutton already had their mind made up."

"I personally think that Vito gave Trent an ultimatum- fire you or he loses his job. But I'm going to get to the bottom of this. Expect to get a phone call from Elvis Winter, the Plant Chairperson in the next couple of days. We're going to do everything we can to get your job back, yours and Jessica's."

"How long will that take? Obviously not anytime soon."

"It could take weeks, maybe months to be honest, especially with all the focus on the pandemic. This sucks big time. We already struggle with diversity in the workplace and Sutton fires two Black women in nine days. Coincidence? Hell no. Systemic racism is a virus worse than Covid-19."

I get off the cart and give Kareem a big hug. "Stay safe my friend. I'm proud of the person you've become since our high school days. Keep this fire that you have for racial equality."

"I will, thank you Dre. I really believe you'll be back here, unless you find something better. Our Union needs a sister like you."

Starting my van, I notice how the small number of cars in the parking lot. At least I'm not the only one going home for an extended time period. But when Sutton re-opens, I won't be returning.

Tears flooding down my face, I'm about to drive away when a Sutton truck pulls up next to me. This MF-er knew I was getting fired and waited for me. I grab the mace out of my glove compartment.

"Don't push me, little man," I say as Chris rolls down his window. "Don't. Push. Me."

After I roll down my window I ask, "What the hell do you want Chris?"

"Oh, you can call me Blizzard now," he grins. "Payback is a mother huh, and I didn't even have to resort to violence."

I show him my middle finger and shout, "Go to hell! Stay your ass away from my son!"

"Or else what, Audre? You're gonna be broke soon. I don't have to do a damn thing because Terrell's gonna call me once his wrist is feeling better."

He zooms away before I can respond. I want to chase him down but my body refuses to take action. So I scroll up my window and holler in anger, which causes me to cry uncontrollably.

"HANK! WHY DID YOU HAVE TO LEAVE ME TO DEAL WITH ALL OF THIS? GOD, IF YOU DO EXIST, WHY DID YOU ALLOW MY HUSBAND TO DIE? I CAN'T DEAL WITH THIS! I GOT NO JOB, MY SON IS A CRIMINAL, AND NOW YOU POLLUTE THE WORLD WITH A VIRUS! I DON'T KNOW WHY MY FRIENDS PRAY TO YOU, BUT IF YOU DO EXIST, I NEED ANSWERS RIGHT NOW! RIGHT NOW!"

I release my frustration, gather my emotions and drive away. That prick was right. Terrell started pushing while I was working. Now that I'm unemployed and he can't get a job during quarantine, Terrell will be tempted to call Blizzard again. Yet, I'm in this position because of Terrell's stupid decision to be a pusher.

I really need to talk to Tracey right now, but I refuse to bother her and Simon while they're on a much-needed vacation. What should I do?

"The last thing I need right now is Terrell going to prison, or me going to prison for trying to kill Blizzard," I say to myself while driving.

Thinking about prison, a name comes to mind and I gasp.

"Dwight!" I shout the name of Hank's older brother who is a correctional officer. "Google, call Dwight Wilson!"

A desperate time calls for a desperate measure.

30

AUDRE

"Thank you for everything, Dwight. You did so much to help us with the funeral. I owe you," I said as we hugged each other.

"You owe me nothing Audre," he said. *"If you or my nephews need anything, please contact me. I don't care what it is. The least I can do for my brother's legacy, is help you anyway that I can. I'm serious, sis."*

"I know you are. Hopefully I won't have to call you for a need but if there's one I'll take the offer. Have a safe flight home."

Never thought I would have to, but I took Dwight's offer. Like my late husband, he's a man of his word. I called him and we came up with a good plan that should lead Terrell back to a straight path for his life.

I come home with some food from our favorite Caribbean restaurant. Curry goat and roti for Tristan, ox-tail with rice and peas for Terrell. I'm not going to tell them that I got fired today. They can enjoy their food, play video games and watch movies until God knows when, and after they fall asleep, I'll make my moves. Because my boys are nighthawks, it's going to be an all-nighter for me.

"OK, WAKE UP BOYS!" I yell in their room at eight in the morning. "TIME TO GET UP NOW!"

Tristan asks, "Why? It's only 8:00am, we're on March Break."

"I don't care. Time to get up."

"Why Mama?"

"Because I said so dammit. Get up now! Terrell, TERRELL!"

I tap Terrell's feet a few times. Kid is still snoring, so I wet his face with a spray bottle.

"What the hell?" snaps a shook-up Terrell.

"Terrell, get up now. Both of you get dressed, brush your teeth and meet me in the kitchen for 8:30. Don't make me have to tell you twice."

Thirty minutes later, Tristan sits down at the table without his twin. "What's going on, Mama?"

"Where's your brother? TERRELL!"

Terrell comes to the kitchen pulling a shirt over his casted wrist. "Mama, where are all my good clothes?"

I answer, "They were in the wash. Sit down."

"What's this all about, Mama?"

"I was fired from my job yesterday."

Both look at me in shock.

"What? Why Mama?" asks Terrell.

Tristan asks, "Yeah why Mama? You've only been there for two months."

"Do you wanna know why Tristan?" I ask in a calm tone. "How about you ask your twin why I was fired?"

They look at each other confused, then face me again.

Terrell mutters, "Huh? Mama, I have no idea why you-"

"Terrell, who's Blizzard?" I interrupt. "And if you don't answer I will slap the truth outta you."

"He's, he's the person I owe nine hundred dollars."

"And why do you owe him nine hundred dollars?"

"Um, because um, because-"

I reach across the table and slap him hard across the face. "WHY DO YOU OWE HIM NINE HUNDRED BUCKS?"

Startled and shocked, he cries, "Cuz I did a run for him but somebody broke into my school locker and stole it!"

"Drug delivery?"

"Yes," he whispers.

"I CAN'T HEAR YOU!"

"Yes, Mama!"

"Hmmm. So how do you plan on paying this Blizzard guy back? How are you going to come up with nine hundred dollars? And if you struggle to answer me, I'll slap you again!"

"I promised to do another run for him to pay the debt!"

"Oh. Okay son," I say with a reduced volume in my voice. "So instead of learning from your stupid ways and leaving the drug game, you agreed to stay involved in criminal activity. Wow Terrell. Your father would be so proud of you if he was alive."

I know I threw a dagger with that sarcastic statement, but I can't show any mercy right now. Terrell's eyes are flooded and his nose is runny.

"Mama," Tristan says, "Terrell really needed new shoes for basketball and we couldn't afford it, so-"

"Pardon me?" I snap. "Tristan, I know you feel bad for your brother now, but did you just hear the crap that just came out of your mouth? We can't afford a new pair of basketball shoes, so that gives your brother the right to be a drug pusher?"

"I didn't mean-"

"We need a house, so does that mean I should rob a bank? If you don't have any wise things to say or ask, then just SHUT UP!"

Tristan, the more sensitive of the two, lowers his head. Looks like he wants to cry but he stays silent.

"Well Terrell, let me tell you why my termination is your fault. It's your fault because you chose to make money the illegal way with a guy named Blizzard, who's actual name is Chris Silverman. He also happens to work in the same department as your mother at the Sutton Assembly Plant! It's your fault because he kicked the crap out of you because you owed him money and I had to take out more than an entire paycheck to cover your debt. Now, I'm more behind on the main bills. It's your fault because seeing you wounded because of a stupid ass decision you made led me to deal with his ass in the parking lot of where I worked, which led me to getting fired! Do you dare to disagree?"

"No," Terrell sobs. "I'm sorry Mama for everything. I'll get a real job and pay you back, I promise."

"Mmm hmmm. Get a real job during the pandemic and we're on lockdown? Okay."

I hear the doorbell ring.

"Tristan, answer the door," I say while getting up to go to my bedroom, trying not to break into tears. *Dre, you can do this.*

"What's with the luggage, Mama?" Tristan asks as he looks at everyone for an answer. Will is sitting down at the table, munching an apple to avoid answering his nephew. Terrell appears nervous but tries to look tough in the presence of his uncle.

I say, "Terrell, remember in the hospital I said there will be consequences if you refused to give me info on who did this to you?"

"Yes," he replies.

"If you weren't injured right now, my guess is that even during this pandemic you would try to get out of the house and be involved with something you shouldn't be doing, like pushing drugs. You may be sorry for what you did but I can't trust that you won't go back to Blizzard when the money struggle is greater, and you can't find a job.

Remember the times when your Uncle Dwight would visit and we would always laugh about where he lives? How y'all would say 'I could never go there, it's too damn boring'? Well karma kicked you in the ass, son. You're going to stay with your Uncle Dwight in Birch Hills, Saskatchewan."

"WHAT? Are you serious, Mama?"

Tristan asks, "You're joking right?"

I say, "Your Uncle Dwight is a correctional officer at the Saskatchewan Penitentiary and lives in a very small town. Lots of land, little crime, and no thugs unless he takes you to the jail to meet some of the inmates. He's planning an agenda for you as we speak."

Terrell asks, "What about school and basketball? My injuries and trying to heal?"

"You're on an extended March Break. Schools are shutdown so who knows when they are starting again. If the NBA season is on hold right now, you definitely know high school basketball is not happening. All the medical supplies you need are already packed and Uncle Dwight will arrange appointments for you with his family doctor."

"How am I getting there?"

"By plane. Your flight is at noon."

"TODAY?" both twins ask in disbelief.

I answer, "You're packed and ready to go. Uncle Will is driving you to the airport. Tristan, you can go to the airport and spend the next couple of hours with your brother."

Terrell asks, "How long am I going there for?"

"To be determined," I answer. "It's a one-way ticket. You will come home once Uncle Dwight believes that you're ready to make wise life decisions."

"Mama, I'm already changed! I won't go back to pushing, I-"

"Your Uncle Will paid for this flight, so if you miss this plane, I will do more than what Blizzard did to you."

Will says, "Your mother had a good paying job and never made it past probation. What she did to that guy at work and what she's doing now is because of her love for you and Tristan."

"I'm sorry, but this is asinine Mama!" Tristan snaps.

"Excuse me?" I snap back.

"If Dad was here, he wouldn't-"

"IF YOUR DAD WAS HERE, TERRELL WOULDN'T HAVE EVEN THOUGHT ABOUT SELLING DRUGS! I MADE THIS DECISION BECAUSE THIS IS WHAT'S BEST FOR TERRELL TO CHANGE HIS LIFE! JUST BE THANKFUL YOU'RE NOT GOING WITH HIM!"

A tear drops as I gaze at Terrell's face that's pleading me to change my mind.

"I love you Terrell. And I want to believe that you'll make me proud of you again. Will, you can take him now."

Terrell calls my name twice as I walk to my bedroom and shut the door. If I give him a hug and kiss, I may cancel the flight. As I lie face down on my bed with a pillow over my head, I cry uncontrollably until I eventually fall asleep.

31

JESSICA

March 25, 2020

    My body is starting to heal a little quicker since I was fired over two weeks ago. The kids really are enjoying me being home all the time now, and it's even better now with Darian home because of the lockdown. My husband loves it because he now has a ton of opportunities to get some writing done for his novel series and spoken-word poetry. As for me, I'm learning how to make videos for YouTube to promote my make-up business and do skin care tutorials.

    I'm also spending more time reading the Word and praying, but it hasn't been easy. When I think about the day I was terminated, bitterness and anger consume my thoughts. Elvis Winter, the Plant Chairperson, called me the day after saying that he will try to get me re-hired with my lost wages and my ninety days restored. I'm not holding my breath, especially with the pandemic shutting almost everything down. Also, I don't know the difference between lies and truth when it comes to Management and Union executives at Sutton.

    "Hun, if you need me, I'll be on the balcony doing some writing," Darian says while I'm watching The Office on Netflix.

"Ok," I reply. "Hey, when are Simon and Tracey returning from Dubai?"

"They came back last night. They're at Tracey's brother's house to get the twins and driving home tonight."

"Ok cool. I'll text her tomorrow."

My phone rings and it brings a smile to my face. "Audre."

"Jessica, how are you hun?"

"I'm good. You've been in my heart all week and I was planning to call you."

"I've been meaning to call you for the last couple of weeks. I'm sorry to hear what happened to you."

"Dre, don't apologize. The world's been turned upside down this month. I'm so sorry to hear you were let go. How are you doing?"

"Truth be told, Jess... I feel like I'm falling apart."

Audre explains why she got fired in full detail, including what took place in the HR office. Afterwards, I told her what went down during my termination meeting. "Dre, I wish Kareem represented me in my meeting. I swear it felt like the Union wasn't in the room, they were so quiet."

"Kareem did an amazing job, but the end result was the same as yours. Another Black woman played by the White executive. Crazy sh-oops sorry I didn't mean to cuss. I know you're a Christian."

I laugh. "It doesn't mean you have to step on eggshells around me, hun. So, how did your son react to you getting fired?"

"Terrell was sorry, but I had to make him pay. I sent him to Saskatchewan where my late husband's brother lives. He's a man's man that gonna whip his ass in shape; physically and mentally."

"Wow Dre, you don't play!" I say, very impressed with her tough love towards her boys.

"But next to burying my husband, it was the hardest thing I've ever done. I miss Terrell so much. Tristan has been depressed because he misses his twin, and he's upset at me so we barely talk now. All I do now is watch Netflix, drink wine, smoke a blunt, and sleep. It really feels like my life is falling apart and I've failed as a mother."

160

"Not at all, Dre. You're in this position because you're a great mother. You put your job on the line to defend your son and pay his debt. You punishing Terrell by sending him to your brother-in-law, is tough love to make him become a responsible young man."

"Then why do I feel this way?"

"It happens. From a different perspective, I applied for the Sutton job and prayed to get it because we needed a second steady income. Six weeks before I got hire, a truck hits me while jogging and I could've died. Still being able to work at Sutton was a miracle but I had several sick days, one of the reasons I was fired.

I'm still bitter about being fired and I ask God why it happened, and then I remember in the Word that says *Trust in the Lord with all your heart and don't lean on your own understanding. In all ways look up to Him and He will direct your path.* I don't understand why we go through crazy stuff like family problems, financial struggle, physical pain, this pandemic- but I just trust God for a victory, whenever or however that may be. God's timing is always perfect."

There is a lengthy pause, which makes me think there's a lost signal. "Audre, you still there?"

"Yes, yes sorry," she says. "Was just thinking about what you're saying. I'm glad that's how you feel about trusting God. To be honest, me and Him aren't cool like that. Don't know if we'll ever be. I haven't been pleased with Him since Hank got cancer."

"No matter how you feel about God, I promise you, He loves you very much, Dre."

"Well, can you tell God to let me know that's how he feels about me?"

I hear Audre sniffing, so I feel led for my next step. "Here's a better idea. Do you mind if I pray for you right now?"

"No not at all. Lead the way," she agrees.

After shutting off the TV, I pray that Audre receives financial provision and employment during and after the lockdown. I also pray for her boys, and Audre's strength to be a successful single mother.

Audre is crying throughout the prayer and I feel the presence of God moving the entire time.

"Amen," Audre repeats after me. "Thank you, Jessica. That felt good."

I say, "That's the peace of the Lord. He just wants you to trust Him."

"I'll try. Man, now I know why Tracey is a more spiritual woman now. You be rubbing that faith on her."

I grin. "I can't take any of the credit for that. That's all God."

"True. Speaking of Trace, she's on her way home now. We three need to have a 'waiting to exhale' night. You down with- oh damn, this pandemic."

"We can sit six feet apart and bring our own food, no big deal. Oh, but Tracey has to self-isolate for two weeks, right?"

"Another roadblock. This virus only been here for under a month and I'm tired of this already."

I laugh, "Hopefully it's gone by summer."

"For real. Hey, if you're not busy let's call Tracey now. Group chat."

"I'm good. Let's do it."

32

TRACEY

"Ladies, you know I'm down but we gotta do a two-week self-isolation," I say to Audre and Jessica on a three-way call. "As much as I love my home, that's too long. Crazy thing is, the cases in Dubai are much lower than what we have here."

Jessica says, "Well, I guess we'll have to do the Zoom thing until then."

"That video chat app? Ok, whatever," Audre says. "How was your trip, hun?"

"It was really nice, Dubai is a spectacular city," I say. "I mean, it sucks that the cruise was cancelled but we're getting a full refund so we'll do a raincheck when this BS is over. Simon and I relaxed like never before. We also 'worked out' like never before if you know what I mean."

Audre says, "Yes, we know what you mean but it's best you switch the topic really quick, cuz the last thing I wanna do is go on some damn Tinder app."

We chat for a good twenty minutes or so, which helps to kill time on the drive home. Simon is driving while the twins are fast asleep in the backseat. They both share the details of their termination and it angers me, but it warms my heart that they are developing a good friendship.

"Hey I'm almost home, so Jess set up the Zoom meeting for tomorrow," I say. "Love y'all, see you soon."

Ending the phone call, I caress my husband's back as he's driving. "You good baby?"

Simon says, "Jet lag is hitting hard, but I'm great. This break is better than I thought it would be, especially when it seemed like it might be a disaster. After finding out the cruise was cancelled, I was so disappointed I was like 'forget this trip, let's stay home'." But Dubai was great as a getaway and hanging out with the church family."

"Yeah, Pastor Marvin and Tammy were a joy to be around. The conversations were so good."

"Definitely. The trip was a blessing. Now, we're home and we have to self-isolate, which isn't a big deal because our plan next week was to chill at home anyway."

"God is so good."

"And after this quarantine, I still don't have to go back to work because Sutton may be closed until Easter at minimum. God is good indeed."

"Well, after we self-isolate I'm back at work. I'm gonna take full advantage of being at home. Play with the kids. Cook some dishes. Try to read some of the books we bought years ago. Just to relax and not be a cop for two more weeks is a blessing. Oh yeah, can't forget some Zoom time with my girls. They were there for me during the O'Malley mess, and my girls, more so Audre could use a positive boost right now."

"Yeah, Dre's a strong woman but she's dealing with a lot. And the twins are good kids. They will get through this stronger. We just gotta keep praying for them. Same with Darian and Jessica. Damn, where would we be right now if they didn't invite us to church last year?"

"I think about that all the time. It blows my mind that we've gone this long without drinking, even on our vacation. That's all God in my opinion."

"No doubt. Although I was tempted numerous times in Dubai, my mind quickly focused on why I no longer need to consume alcohol."

"Your change has been an incredible story babe. Keep trusting God, keep pushing. Oh, when I return to work it will feel like a fresh new start to my career. I'll be refreshed physically, mentally and spiritually. I can't wait to sleep in our own bed tonight."

He laughs, "I was just going to say that! Man, it's calling me right now!"

We finally pull into our driveway. I have never been so excited to see our home. Our traveling is over and now the real relaxation begins.

Simon puts the car in park. "The kids are still sleeping. I'm just going to quickly run in because I need to pee really bad."

I sigh. "Ok hurry up, I need to go too."

"Sorry babe. Gimme two minutes."

If the twins were awake, I would just unbuckle their seat belts and head on inside. When Simon returns, we'll each lift up a child and unload the luggage.

My phone is buzzing. It's my amazing partner who I haven't spoken to since my last work day. "Harpreet, what's good?"

"Tracey, I wasn't going to call you during your vacation," he answers, sounding serious.

"No worries, what's going on? I missed ya, bro."

"Missed you too. I'm outside of the supermarket near my house and my car is covered in hot liquid feces."

"What the hell?" I get out of my car to avoid waking up the kids with my raised voice.

"The stench is so horrific I wanna throw up. And on the hood is white spray paint saying 'Step Down Paki'. Liam is on his way to investigate this so I'm giving you a heads up. We're being targeted."

"Somebody tied to O'Malley," I say while looking in all directions trying to find anything out of the ordinary.

"If anything else comes up I'll contact you. I'm sure you'll hear from Liam shortly."

I let out a big sigh, "Ok. How are you feeling? I can only imagine what's going on in your head right now."

"Words can't express the anger I'm feeling at this moment. Not just the hate or that my car is ruined, but if this is tied with O'Malley, the belief that these racists will defend a deranged pervert like him is beyond disgusting."

As Harpreet is talking, Simon rushes out the house towards me and says, "Get in the car. We're going to a hotel."

I say, "What?"

"Get in the car!"

Harpreet asks, "You alright Tracey?"

"Harpreet, let me call you back," I say while angrily staring at my husband. "Simon, what the hell is going on? Why are we going to a hotel?"

"Baby, I'm begging you, don't go in the house!"

"Simon, I'm going in to see what's going on. I just got off the phone with Harpreet. Is it hate-related?"

"YES! What's going on, Trace?"

I take my gun from the glove compartment and head to the front door.

"TRACEY, YOU'LL REGRET GOING IN! DON'T GO..."

The moment I open the door a noose is hanging from the ceiling in the hallway.

Black spray paint is on the wall of the hallway with the words STEP DOWN NIGGER.

The living room has a confederate flag on the sofa. Our wedding photo has a sketching of a gun next to my head. On the wall above the fireplace, it reads NIGGER KIDS with arrows pointing to the photos of Symon and Symone.

The kitchen is surprisingly not vandalized.

A horrific stench is coming from upstairs. It's coming from the kids' washroom. The toilet is clogged and above it the wall reads NIGGERS ARE WORSE THAN with an arrow pointing to the putrid feces. GOD'S CURSE is written on the mirror and I happen to be right under it. Immediately, I smash the mirror with my gun.

"Don't fu- don't mess with me, Satan!" I growl. "Jesus, why is this happening?"

I enter the Master Bedroom. Above the headboard of our king-size bed, the words STOP PRODUCING NIGGERS are big and bold.

My husband is right. I regret entering our once lovely and blessed home. Especially after I view the twin's bedroom.

Two miniature nooses hanging above their beds.

The anger in me is so powerful that it draws me to my knees. "JESUS!" I yell from the top of my lungs.

Sobbing and screaming, I've been pushed to my limit. Whoever did this, I'm ready to kill them.

33

SKITTLES

"I put you on Face Time so you can see that I'm wearing a mask and gloves," I say to Donna on my iPhone. "My dad also got a glass screen installed over the counter yesterday. I'm sanitizing every time the store is free of customers."

"Good. We're finally going to be together tonight and no Covid is coming in my house. Stay safe because I can't wait to be next to you again."

"After seeing each other six days a week from January to mid-March, the last eight days have felt like a month. So, I'm definitely ready to smell your lovely fragrance again and then some."

"And then some," Donna grins. "Dylan just left with the kids so I'm just cleaning up the crib. Damn, why are they so messy?"

"I'm looking forward to meeting them one day."

"One day, but not today. You're all mine. See you later."

"Bye. Oh hey, do you need a pack of toilet paper? We have tons of it here, but not for long."

"No, I'm ok, I bought some two days ago. Make sure you bring some Skittles again. Tropical flavor."

"Girl, you making me sweat. I'm out."

Because my folks are at high-risk of getting the virus, I've been running the store from 7:00 am to 7:00 pm every day since Sutton closed. It has its slow times and steady times but today we expect it to get busy. My father, Jacob Persaud, managed to get a shipment of quality toilet paper which has been scarce in North America since the pandemic. How does Covid make one use more toilet paper than usual? Still trying to figure that out.

I really miss seeing my crew because I'm one who doesn't like to be alone for an extended period of time. My parents and I are under the same roof but be stay distanced from each other because I'm around customers all day. Zoom is okay as well as Face Time but it's not the same. Hanging out with Donna is going to feel so good.

I'm still waiting for my boy to text me back. Simon and Tracey came home yesterday as far as I know. Maybe they're still recovering from jet lag. I miss my Harrison fam.

I really miss Audre too. So much has changed for her since we last saw each other. I'm beyond upset that she got fired for defending her son on the company's parking lot. Terrell, who I consider my adopted nephew, acted stupid and deserves the punishment he's receiving. I have to make a mental note to send him and Tristan an encouragement text to stay strong and be a help to their mother as much as possible. I decide to put together for her a care package: toilet paper, Lysol wipes, paper towels, and hand sanitizer, which I'll drop to her apartment tomorrow morning.

My dad comes into the store and says, "Son, the truck should be here in an hour with the toilet paper. Make sure you price it for fifteen dollars."

"Damn Pops, that's too high," I say. "I know this is a convenience store but that's too much for a dozen rolls."

"Eddie, toilet paper is sold out everywhere right now. They will sell out quick."

"Yes Pops, but all it takes is one customer to complain and put a photo of the price on social media. If this store gets called out for price gouging that's not good for business."

He sighs. "Ok. Thirteen dollars."

"Ten dollars, Pop."

"Thirteen."

"Ten."

"12.99."

"Really, Pop? Ok $10.99, how about that?"

Sighing again, he nods his head. "I have another request Eddie. Can you open the store and work until noon tomorrow? Your cousin can't make it in the morning."

"Pop, I have plans tonight because I thought I wasn't needed until five."

"I know it's last minute but if you can do it, I'll give you Saturday off."

Now it's my turn to sigh. My plan was to stay overnight at Donna's, but now I will have to leave much earlier than anticipated.

"Ok, I'll do it. And I'll still work on Saturday."

My dad says, "No son, you don't have to do Saturday, I'll come in."

"I'm good, Pop. Your high risk, and all I'll be doing is staying home anyway if I don't come in."

"Thank you, son. Your mother made some Doubles for you this morning so I'll put in the kitchen for you."

After he leaves, I waste no time to warm up some authentic Trini Doubles with pepper and tamarind sauce. Feeling a buzz, I pull out my phone to see if Simon returned my text. Nope, it's just another email from another business telling me to stay safe.

"Ok, I know a good game that will get us to know each other better," Donna says after setting up the Chromecast on her TV. "Let's play 'One's Gotta Go.'"

After a very delicious meal prepared by Donna, it's close to nine in the evening and we're in the family room having wine and snacks. The night is still young and we are both feeling a buzz and very comfortable.

"Alright, I've played it a few times while scrolling through Facebook. Let's go," I reply.

"Ok, here's the first screen: IG, Netflix, Google, and YouTube. One's gotta go."

"Hmmm, I'm not sure. Which one would you eliminate?"

"Probably IG. I have an account but I barely use it. The other three I use every day."

"I see. For me, Netflix will have to go."

"Netflix? Every time I call you at home, you're binge watching The Umbrella Academy or Breaking Bad."

"Yeah, I love Netflix, but when it comes to self-promotion Netflix can't help me. The other three can."

"Ahh, good logic," Donna says. "Ok let's go to music. I know you love Michael Jackson. His albums- Off the Wall, Thriller, Bad, Dangerous. One's gotta go."

"Dammm!" I shout. "How you gonna go there, bae? I love all of them!"

"One's gotta go, Skid. Which one?"

"Man. Off the Wall is a straight up classic. You gotta be insane to eliminate Thriller, the most successful album of all time. So, for me it comes to down to Bad or Dangerous. Oh boy. Bad's gotta go."

"Really, Bad?" Donna asks. "Bad has tons of good songs, like Man in the Mirror, The Way You Make Me Feel, Smooth Criminal."

I haven't listened to Smooth Criminal since Tucker Mayfield. Bad memories.

"I chose Bad because Michael and Quincy Jones had the pressure of living up the success of Thriller and it was near impossible. Not as good as expected."

"But it's still a great album. My choice is Dangerous."

"Strongly disagree. If you listen to Dangerous from start to finish, it's an underrated masterpiece. 'Jam' may be Michael's more slept-on song ever."

Donna doesn't respond. She lets out a loud sigh. "Really, Dylan? Why now?"

"What is it?"

"Dylan is outside. Our daughter, Emma, forgot her stuffed hippo which she always has to have before bedtime. I don't want him inside so I'll take it to him."

The doorbell rings. Suddenly I feel stressed. I'm in no mood for any drama or tension and I don't want Donna's mood to change either.

"This will be quick," she says as she goes to the door. "You're smart to wear a mask, Dylan. Wait there, I'll go and get Lulu."

As Donna runs upstairs to get the hippo for her daughter, I decide to get up from the sofa and walk to the entrance. Dylan starts to approach me.

"Hey Eddie, I really haven't properly introduced myself. Dylan. I would shake your hand but-"

His politeness comes as a surprise. "No worries, social distancing. Good to meet you."

"I apologize for being a jerk at the restaurant a couple of months ago. After that night, my friend Tucker told me how he pulled you over and my judgment of you wasn't positive, even though you don't have a criminal record."

"Still don't."

"Right, right. So for the love of my kids, I have to trust that their mother won't date anyone who's a bad influence. Here's to a new start."

"New start," I agree, feeling a monkey lifting off my back about Dylan's possible dislike of me. It's still way too early to trust him.

"Hey, I noticed you drive a Charger. What year is your model?"

"Uh, 2007."

"Oh ok. I have a 2018. I also assemble them because I work at the FCA Plant in Brampton. You work with Donna at Sutton, right?"

"Yeah, the Engine Line. What area do you work?"

"Pick and Pack. I don't know what they call it at Sutton, but I load the necessary parts in a cart for the assemblers in Final. One of the parts is the key FOB. I'm curious, can I see your key FOB? I wanna see how different they look from 2007 to now."

Donna returns and looks at us with suspicion. "Is everything alright here?"

I answer, "Yeah, we're just talking cars. Bae, can I get a Lysol wipe, please?"

"Uh, sure." She gives Dylan the stuffed animal and gives him a look before going to the half washroom.

I took out my keys from my jacket pocket, which he takes and compares it with his key FOB. Dylan explains the changes in the two FOBs, such as the wider shape of his newer FOB and that it's also keyless. Dylan returns it to me and I sanitize the keys with the Lysol wipe.

"There you go," says Dylan. "New or old, the Charger is freaking amazing."

"I agree. Gotta love anything with a HEMI engine," I say.

Donna asks, "I'm glad you both are getting along, but don't you have to get back to my kids?"

"Going now," Dylan answers. "Emma won't go to sleep without it. Nice meeting you, Eddie. Stay safe."

"Same to you," I say.

Donna closes the door and I return to the living room after washing my hands. "Ok, no more interruptions, although I'm pleased that Dylan wasn't a jerk towards you."

"Yeah, thank God," I say. "So, what were we doing, One's Gotta Go right?"

"Yeah, but let's go upstairs. I'm ready for Taste the Rainbow."

I want to sleep all night and throughout the morning as anticipated, but I promised to open the store for my father. Lying next to this warm, sexy body has got me thinking if I can eventually marry Donna. I have yet to tell her that I love her because we still want to take things slow in our relationship. However, sex has already defeated that plan. I guess we'll really have to see how we get through this pandemic as a couple.

"I wish you didn't have to leave so soon," Donna pleads as she walks me to the front door. "Please say you'll come back later."

"I'm only working at the store until noon, so maybe I'll reach around two or three this afternoon," I confirm. "I'll bring some food too. You like roti?"

"Don't judge me if I say I have yet to try it."

"What? You've never had roti? Well, today is your day to try it. If you like curry then you'll love roti. Damn, I could eat one now."

"I can't wait. Be safe at work."

"I will." We hug and share a passionate kiss. "See you soon."

As the engine is warming up, I place my phone on the holder and make sure the music that I want to hear is on display. I no longer touch my phone while driving. Because of only a few hours of sleep, I want a song loaded with energy and the one that comes to mind is "Jam" by the late King of Pop.

"One, two, three," I repeat as the song begins, leaving the driveway. I absolutely love the long one-minute intro as it quickly energizes me. My head is nodding, hands tapping the steering wheel.

No pun intended, I'm jamming hard at five in the morning, reciting the entire first verse word-for-word. With little to no traffic on the roads, I still stay under the speed limit, which is hard to do with a HEMI engine muscle car.

I see that McDonald's isn't busy, so I decide to go to the Drive-Thru for a couple of breakfast sandwiches, singing verse two until I reach the menu and speaker board.

"The world keeps changing, rearranging minds and thoughts, predictions fly of doom, the baby boom has come of age, we'll I work it out. I told my brother don't you ask me for no favors. I'm conditioned by the system, don't you talk to me, don't scream and shout."

I turn the music down.

The voice box asks, "Welcome to McDonald's, can I take your order?"

"Two sausage egg muffins please."

"That's it?"

"Yes please."

"Drive up."

I scroll up the window, turn up the volume and shout the chorus.

After paying and getting my food, I see a police car in the parking lot. It's not going through the Drive-Thru lane. I shrug my shoulders and drive away. I turn up the volume again to join the late Heavy D with his eight-bar verse.

After the rap, I don't sing the chorus. A police car is driving behind me. Don't ask me why, because I'm not violating any rules.

"It ain't too hard for me to jam," I sing while looking at the rear-view mirror. *"It ain't too hard for me to jam, it ain't too hard for-"*

The lights are flashing.

"Why Lord?" I cry as I pull my car to the roadside. "Lord, please let this be quick because I've done nothing wrong."

Scrolling down the window as the cop approaches me, he says, "Hello, can I see your license and ownership please?"

First thing I do is memorize his badge number. "Yes sir," I comply and open the glove compartment to grab my information.

"Is this your car, sir?" he asks after taking it.

"Yes, I'm Edward Persaud. May I ask why I'm being pulled over?"

"It's early morning and your music is pretty loud. Just making sure you haven't been drinking."

Thank God I only had one drink of wine and it was eight hours ago, so I'm very sober.

"Where are you coming from?" he asks.

"A friend's house, sir."

"Shouldn't you be in your own home to prevent the spread of the virus?"

"We're dating, sir."

Another flashing car arrives. Now I really want to know what the hell is going on.

The cop asks, "Where are you going now?"

"To work, sir."

"And where is that?"

"Jake's Variety. It's ten minutes away from here."

A second cop arrives by my front passenger window. Both are White. I memorize his badge number as well.

"Sir, can you open your trunk? We need to do a search in your vehicle," he says.

I say, "Sure, I have nothing to hide."

I pull the trunk lever and the second cop opens the decklid while the first cop stays by my window. The easier I cooperate, the sooner they leave. I'm so frustrated of being pulled over but I'm holding in my emotions. Instead, I'm praying under my breath and being polite.

Cop two stands next to cop one and says, "Can you tell me why there's a fully loaded handgun in your trunk?"

A wave of shock enters my body. "What? Loaded handgun? I don't own a gun."

"This is your vehicle, correct?"

"Yes, but I don't own a gun."

"Then why is there a gun in your trunk?"

"I don't know, I don't own a gun!" I snap.

Cop one says, "Step out the car, sir."

"For what? I don't own a-"

He swings the door open and pulls me out by my hair. "I SAID GET OUT OF THE CAR!"

"WHAT THE HELL? LET GO OF MY HAIR!"

"Get your ass over here," Cop two orders as Cop one tells me to place my hands on the roof of my car.

"Jesus help me," I whisper.

Cop two shows me the silver handgun which I have never seen before. "Can you tell me why the hell you have a loaded 38 caliber revolver in your trunk?"

"Officer, I've never seen that gun before!" I argue as Cop one pats me down. "The only thing I thought was in my trunk was some cleaning products I'm giving to a friend!"

Cop two slams my head on the roof. "Listen to me, you pussy! You better stop lying to me now before you really feel my anger!"

"I'M NOT LYING! I'VE NEVER-"

Cop one asks, "Is this your car, Edward?"

"I already told you this is my car, but that's not my gun!"

Cop two growls, "ARE YOU THINKING THAT WE WOULD JUST STOP YOU AT RANDOM AND PLACE A DAMN GUN IN YOUR CAR?"

"No, but somebody had to because I-"

My mind flashes back to Dylan holding my key FOB.

"You trying to think of another lie?"

"I'M NOT LYING! I'M BEING SET UP!"

"Heard this story one too many times," Cop one says as he aggressively pulls my arms behind my back. "You are under arrest for possessing a firearm. You have the right to remain silent-"

"I WILL NOT REMAIN SILENT! I AM AN INNOCENT BLACK MAN WHO'S NEVER DONE ANY CRIME! RELEASE ME NOW!"

Cop two punches me across the face. I should've stayed silent.

"Your new home will be behind bars with the other thugs like you."

"GO TO HELL!"

Next thing I know, I'm on the ground yelling in pain as a club strikes multiple times across my back.

34

SIMEON

"Did you park down the street?" I ask my friend Marla when I let her in through the side entrance.

She replies, "Yeah, a block away."

"Cool, follow me." We quietly went downstairs to my large room in the basement. Quiet because I'm not allowed to have any visitors during this pandemic, but a brother got needs.

"Oooh, a cozy stand-up shower," Marla says, looking at the washroom attached to my bedroom. "You wanna go there or your bed?"

"Hmmm, we need to get rid of our germs anyway," I say while taking off my shirt. "Let's get wet."

A half hour later while I'm putting on my clothes, Marla is forming rows of coke on my end table.

"What the hell, you can't do that in here!" I snap. "I'm not even supposed to have anybody over, so you gotta bounce."

"C'mon, just one quick hit after a great orgasm," she begs.

"Nah you gotta go. I don't want my mom to rip me a new one. Besides, I stopped taking blow, only weed now."

"You're a bad liar. I'll leave some here for you. Walk me out, please."

I walk Marla to her car and return minutes later. Going to the kitchen to grab a plate of leftovers before I play more PS4.

"What the hell is wrong with you?"

I jump. "Dammit Mom, you scared the hell outta me!"

Mom says, "You're still bringing your thots to this house? You don't know where the hell they been or who they been in contact with, yet you touching them all up?"

"Mom-"

"Do you not realize we are in a lockdown for a reason? This is a pandemic, Simeon. Your father and I are at a higher risk of getting sick than you are. Your horny ass can have the virus right now! This is my house, your dad's house, our safe haven and I don't wanna wear a mask in my damn house because you can't stay home!"

"I'm sorry Mom! I'll be more careful, I promise."

"Get the wipes and sanitize everything y'all just touched. Here's a new hashtag for you young people: hashtag stay-yo-ass-home!"

While grabbing the cleaning supplies from under the sink, she asks, "Have you heard from your brother yet?"

"No," I answer. "Simon said he'll text me when he needs his truck back. He's not rushing now since we're not going back to work soon."

"Ok. They're probably still recuperating from the jet lag. I'll text him tomorrow. Good night."

"Night Mom."

This lockdown feels good and pisses me off at the same time. It's nice to know that I'm home without being sick or unemployed. It sucks to be off work and unable to enjoy life outside the house. It's only been a week and I'm already getting tired of smoking weed, playing video games and watching porn. I stopped taking blow for almost two months but I'm tempted to use what Marla left me. Maybe later.

My cleaning is done and I'm about to log onto my PS4 when my phone rings. It's not one of my saved numbers. "Hello."

"Simmy Love, Simmy Simmy Simmy Love!"

"Nezzie?"

"Of course baby, it's your bae, it's your sexy bae."

"How are you doing?"

"Ohhh, I'm so happy to hear your sexy voice. I've been so miserable without you."

Nezzie sounds like she drunk and off her meds. Suddenly my walls are a deck of cards ready to come down.

"I miss you too," I say. "Did you get a new phone number?"

"Yes, I did and I didn't have your number because my brother destroyed my sim card. But yesterday I found your number on the piece of paper that I wrote it on the day I met you. That's fate, Simmy Love. That's desstineee."

"So how are you feeling? Are you still on med-"

"Simmy, can you come over please? I really need you right now."

I have to rebuild my walls again because I refuse to get sucker-punched again.

"You're doing it again, Nezzie."

"Doing what?"

"We got back together and you only wanted to see me when you weren't on medication. I never hear from you when you're taking your medicine. Why not?"

"That's because those nasty-ass pills turn my brain into mush, and then I don't know what I want when I'm on them."

"And the last time you called me to come over, your family confronted me. I'm not falling for that again Nezzie."

"That's not gonna happen, I promise. Please Simmy, please come over, I need you."

"I don't believe you. What if your brother is tracking this phone now? Sorry Nez."

"Please Sim! I promise you my family won't find out!"

180

"Really Nez? And why is that? Gimme one good reason why?"

"My family has Covid!"

Now she's sobbing and my heart is melting for her.

"You serious? Your whole family?"

"Yes, my parents and my brother. They just found out today."

"When's the last time you were with them?"

"Not since early March, so I'm ok. I'm so scared Simmy, I don't want them to die!"

"They're not going to die, Nezzie."

"How do you know that? So many people in Italy are dying from this virus. Now it's over here and people are dying! I can't go through this alone, Simmy, because I'm afraid I'll do something stupid!"

"Stupid like what?"

"I don't know, like harm myself or something, but when I'm with you everything seems better. Please come over Simmy, please!"

Damn. This is only moments after Mom scolding me. I hate to get on her bad side, but if I don't see Nezzie, self-harm may happen.

"Are you home?" I ask.

"Yes, come now."

It doesn't take long for me to get a text from my parents after leaving the driveway.

DAD

Where the hell are you going? Why do you choose to stress out your mother?

ME

Sorry Dad, I got an emergency call from my friend

DAD

What friend?

I'm not trying to have another argument at this moment. I'll deal with the consequences later.

Arriving at her apartment building, I text Nezzie to let her know I'm here.

NEZZIE

Come to the roof.

Take the stairs.

"Da hell is this woman up to?" I ask myself as I park the truck in the visitor's spot and open the back entrance. Her apartment building is old with little security. There are only six floors of steps to climb, and I'm hoping it's just her and I'm not being set up again. It's possible that Nezzie's lying about her family having the virus only to make me come to see her.

Pushing the door open to the wide and flat roof, I see Nezzie near the ledge holding a vodka bottle and smoking a joint. Thankfully she's not on top of the ledge. "Hey," I say as I'm walking to her.

"Simmy Love!" Nezzie drops her joint and puts down her bottle to hug me. She reeks of liquor but it feels so good to embrace her body. It makes me realize that I really did miss her.

After a long kiss I ask, "What are you doing up here?"

Nezzie releases me and says, "I needed to escape. This is where I can be free and give two middle fingers to the world. I don't have to listen or take orders from nobody. Unless of course it's you telling me how to work it."

She starts twerking on me like we're in the club. "You ever had sex on a rooftop, Simmy?"

"Nah," I reply, anticipating another bang within the last two hours.

Nezzie faces me and starts to unzip my pants. "Me neither."

For the next two minutes she's orally satisfying me. I've heard some men say that unstable women give the best sex and I can't agree more. It's one of the reasons why I can't fully move on from Nezzie. Misery loves company and we're a hot mess together.

Suddenly she stops working her magic and starts to cry. "My family is gonna die. I don't want them to die."

"Come," I say with my arms open, knowing that sex isn't going to happen. "They will get through this."

"No, they won't! My mother already has heart problems, my dad has early Alzheimer's and my brother's a diabetic. How are they gonna survive this?"

"I don't know Nezzie. This virus is crazy and I don't have any answers. I'm just trying to be here for you, that's all."

"I know," she says along with a hug. "That's why I love you, Simmy. You're the only one who understands me, like when I need some Blow. You brought me some Blow, baby?"

As if she's not messed up enough right now. It's a rare moment that Nezzie is like this and I'm still sober. To give her Blow and I don't snort any would seem like I'm trying to make her worse. So it's either both of us partake of the powder or nobody has any.

I take out the bag and pour some on my arm for her to snort, and then she returns the favor.

"WOO HOO, I NEEDED THIS!" Nezzie yells. "I need to do something crazy to get my mind off this stupid-ass Covid!"

"What do you wanna do?" I ask. "We can go for a long drive in my brother's truck, escape the craziness of this city. Go to a hick town, crash at a motel and-"

"Nah, that's not crazy. I know what I wanna do."

Nezzie walks to the ledge and steps on it, which shocks the hell out of me.

"WHAT ARE YOU DOING?" I shout. "Get the hell down, what's wrong with you? Get down!"

"Relax Simmy, chill yourself. I took gymnastics as a teenager, so my balance is freaking amazing. Look." She spreads her arms and lifts up her left leg.

"Damn woman, you're scaring the hell outta me! This ain't funny, get down!"

"You're such a chicken. I didn't know you're scared of heights."

"I'm not scared of heights but I don't wanna risk my life walking on the edge of the roof. One little slip and it's over, bae! Get your ass down!"

"Simmy, I'm going through a lot right now and this makes me feel good at the moment! I'm not trying to kill myself, ok?"

"But just because it feels good doesn't mean that you should do it!"

"Says the one who just gave me blow!"

"Point taken, but please just come down!"

"No, I'm fine. Like I said, I was a gymnast so balancing on this is easy. I can easily do this for an hour."

"If people notice you up here, someone's gonna-"

"I don't give a damn what people think, Simmy. If you're gonna be here, then shut the hell up and let me do my thing. If not, get the hell off this roof!"

I didn't know what else to do. My mind was circulating as to how to get Nezzie down. If I pull her off, I'm afraid of the backlash of her doing something crazier. I can join Nezzie on the ledge as "can't beat her join her" gesture, but I'm not trying to draw more attention than the few neighbors already staring at her, and it may be my ass falling off instead of her.

Maybe I can call my sister-in-law, but she's still on vacation and I don't want my family involved with this.

"I BELIEVE I CAN FLY!" she sings with her arms stretched. "I BELIEVE I CAN..."

Nezzie can sing, and it almost makes me forget how pissed I am at her behavior. I stand and watch her sing the entire R. Kelly song. I'm praying to God or whoever exists in the supernatural universe to cause a divine intervention and get my bae off the ledge.

"Ok, did you get your fix on now? You good? Come down Nezzie."

"Why, Simmy? And do what, mope around and cry because my family is dying? I've been up here for ten minutes and I haven't flinched or moved an inch. That's because I got skills baby! I used to kick ass at gymnastics. Right now, I can do a cartwheel no problem but I don't wanna scare your chicken ass. Did I ever tell you how I almost won a gymnastics tournament when I was sixteen?"

"For real? I didn't know that," I lie but it buys me time to figure out a plan to get her off.

"I was killing it, destroying all my competition. But apparently, I was being arrogant and this white girl in the crowd said 'Shut up ho!' I ran so fast into the bleachers and started kicking her ass. Long story short, I got disqualified and months later diagnosed as 'bipolar'.

So for the last fifteen years of my life, I've been known as that crazy unstable Black woman who can't do regular things in life without taking crappy medication. Oh wow Simmy, I just saw a blue jay fly on that tree! Did you see it?"

"No bae, I missed it."

"It was so pretty. Oh dammit, I forgot to set the PVR for Grey's Anatomy. Did you watch it, Simmy?"

"No, I don't watch that show bae."

"Did season three of Stranger Things come out yet?"

"No, it comes out around-"

"Why can't I get that Post Malone song outta my head? What's it called again? Is it 'Runaway'?"

"No, it's called 'Circles'."

"Yes! 'Circles'!" Then she sings the Post Malone hit better than the man himself.

Does Nezzie dare me to do something? Is she waiting on me to make a move?

I don't care if she hates me afterward, but I'm going to pull her down from the ledge. I look down and there's a few people staring with concern, so I need to end their entertainment now. While she's focusing on her singing and not looking at me, I reach out my arms, getting ready to grab her waist and pull. Then, I hear the rooftop door open.

Turning around, I see two police officers slowly approaching us.

"Nezzie, the cops are up here."

She stops singing and turns around. "No way! Was I really singing that loud?"

185

"It's not the singing, people see that you're on the roof and someone called the police thinking you wanna commit suicide."

"Hello, is everything okay here?" asks the officer who's a middle-aged white man.

I hope they don't see the empty bag of coke on the ground.

"Hello officers, we're up here enjoying the breeze," I say. "We're a little tired of being in the house."

The female officer says, "Well, you can go for a walk as another option. We received a call about a person attempting to jump from this building."

Nezzie laughs, "I'm not trying to jump, officers. I'm going to fly, no no, just kidding. I used to be a competitive gymnast and I felt this ledge would be a good area to practice my agility. One day I would like to walk a tightrope and what better way to practice than a ledge that's five stories high-"

I mumble, "Nezzie, enough!"

"Were you guys drinking?" asks the older cop.

"No we weren't, sir."

"Well, one of you reeks of alcohol. Ma'am, I'm going to need you to step down from the ledge before you get hurt."

"How am I going to get hurt, officer?" Nezzie asks. "If I fall, I won't be hurt, I'd be dead. But I'm perfectly fine."

The lady says, "Yes, and we want you to stay that way, so can you please step down?"

"I'm fine, Miss. I'm not breaking any law. Why don't you use your time to catch criminals, because we're good."

"You're actually on private property."

"No we're not. I live in this building and my boyfriend is my guest."

The male officer says, "There's a sign that specifically states no trespassing and that is for tenants as well. So I need you to step down-"

"I'm not stepping down and if you make me, I'll jump, I swear to God!"

Now I'm really scared of what the cops may do to Nezzie. "Bae, just come down. Let's go home."

"I KNOW MY RIGHTS, SIMMY! I'M NOT DOING ANYTHING WRONG!"

The lady asks, "What's your name, ma'am?"

"Inez, but I'm known as Nezzie."

"Nezzie, we are only here to make sure that you are safe. Has this man committed any harm to you whatsoever?"

Pointing to me, she answers, "My Simmy? Absolutely not, he would never hurt me."

"Officer, I got this," the man says to his partner. "Why don't you take this man away so I can talk to Nezzie."

"Take me where, officer?" I cry. "I'm not leaving my girlfriend."

Nezzie begs, "Please don't take my Simmy away!"

He says, "Nothing is going to happen to your boyfriend. Officer Barnabe is only going to take him to the other side of the roof while I talk to you, that's all."

Officer Barnabe doesn't look confident in what her older partner is doing, but she follows command and leads me to the other side of the roof.

"Am I in trouble? I promise you officer, I've done nothing wrong. Nezzie is bi-polar, and I've been trying to get her down. But when she's set on doing something you can't change her mind."

"I believe you," she says. "but Officer Rodgers wants to talk to her privately."

"Why, is he an expert on dealing with mental health victims? What's he gonna say-"

"It will be fine."

She and I are diagonally across from Nezzie and the other cop known as Officer Rodgers. I don't trust these cops at all and I want to know why the hell I'm being pushed aside when all I've been doing is trying to save Nezzie from herself. Thankfully for me, his mask is hanging down as he talks to my woman. I stare directly at his lips,

187

which is difficult because he's about thirty-five feet away, but I mastered this craft for moments like this.

"So I need you to just listen to me carefully for the next couple of minutes, ok? Eyes on me, nothing else," he says to Nezzie.

"Ok," she agrees. Nezzie is surprisingly calm as she stares at the man.

"I believe that you've gone through some difficult times because nobody understands you. It must now be easy to deal with the challenges you've dealt with. Life is so tough and it's even gotten tougher with this pandemic. I know there's someone who loves you, who believes you are unique, smart, and a beautiful Black woman."

If the man is saying what I believe is coming from his lips, it's shockingly admirable considering it's a White male cop. Nezzie is silent and mesmerized when he speaks, as if she's hypnotized.

He continues, "Whoever that someone is, I gotta confess to you sweetheart, it's all lies. Family and friends will say anything to make you feel better because it helps them to deal with you better. You're Black, a female, and you have mental health issues, three things you have going against you. Your life is worthless, Nezzie. It would make everybody's life easier if you just jump off this roof right now."

Horrified at what I'm hearing, I holler, "NEZZIE! DON'T LISTEN TO HIM!"

My scream startles Nezzie to the point that her left foot slips and falls off the ledge.

"HELP! SIMMY!"

"NEZZIE!"

Officer Barnabe holds me back. "Don't panic, he's got her wrist! He's got her!"

"HE'S NOT GONNA SAVE HER! HE TOLD HER TO JUMP! HE FREAKING TOLD HER TO JUMP!"

"Relax, he wouldn't do that!"

"SIMMY!" Nezzie yells again.

I yell, "OFFICER, LET ME GO! I READ HIS LIPS AND HE TOLD HER SHE'S USELESS AND NEEDS TO JUMP!"

"STAY HERE!" Officer Barnabe runs to help.

"AHHHHH!" Nezzie screams. "SIMMY!"

I hear a fading scream.

"DAMMIT!" Officer Rodgers yells, pretending to care as he looks over the building.

"NEZZIE!"

I run down the six flights of stairs faster than I ever ran in my life. Pushed open the back door and I run around to the front of the building.

"NEZZIE! NEZZIE!"

I try to see her and the paramedics are already here. I push through the small crowd and see her unconscious with her eyes open. "NO, NO, NO! NEZZIE! IS SHE, IS SHE..."?

Shock hits me to the point that I'm having difficulty breathing. Paramedic worker gives me a respirator. "I'm so sorry, she didn't survive the fall."

The officers arrive as I'm trying to breathe properly again. But as soon as I see Officer Rodgers, my anger takes over.

"YOU KILLED HER! YOU TOLD HER TO JUMP! YOU TOLD HER TO JUMP!"

Two other cops on the scene hold me back because I ran towards the officer.

"I READ YOUR LIPS! YOU ENCOURAGED HER TO JUMP! YOU'RE GOING TO JAIL FOR THIS, YOU RACIST PIECE OF SH-!"

I lose breath again and I have to put on the respirator again. Officer Rodgers approaches me and says, "Go ahead and try and sue me. Who are they going to believe, myself or a lip-reading junkie?"

He walks away with Officer Barnabe who gives me a look as if she believes me.

After I gain my breath again, I yell to the small crowd outside. "THAT COP, OFFICER RODGERS, IS A RACIST AND HE KILLED MY GIRLFRIEND! OFFICER RODGERS IS HIS NAME! INEZ MARTIN IS THE WOMAN HE TOLD TO JUMP OFF THE BUILDING! INEZ MARTIN!"

As I'm about to yell her name once again, the tears drop and I fall to the ground, wishing I was dead instead of having to tell Nezzie's parents that their only daughter Is gone.

"And you must love the Lord your God with all your heart, all your soul, all your mind, and all your strength. The second is equally important: LOVE YOUR NEIGHBOR AS YOURSELF. No other commandment is greater than these."
 MARK 12: 30-31

"But if you do what is wrong, you will be paid back for the wrong you have done. For God has NO FAVORITES."
 COLOSSIANS 3:25

NOW THAT THEY'VE BEEN PUSHED, WHAT IS THE NEXT MOVE?

BRING THE NOISE

THE POWERFUL CONCLUSION TO
DON'T PUSH ME

COMING SOON

I am trying to avoid eye contact with you now. Not literally, but I know what you're thinking: how dare I leave you with this cliffhanger!

Truth be told, I did not want to write a part two to this story. As I was writing, I fell in love with the characters and I wanted them to have a powerful story. Also, I didn't want this to be a 500-page novel so I had to make a part one and two. As I write this, the plot for part two is still developing. But I guarantee you, the intensity is about to go another level. Stay tuned!

It's time to be transparent with you. Chapter 26 tells how Jessica got fired from Sutton and Darian's angry reaction. This chapter is a true story of what took place between my wife, myself and my current employer. The event occurred in 2017. It was hurtful, disappointing, and a strong example of Systemic Racism. How do I know this? There is a White employee who had MANY sick days during their 90-day probation. Many as in a large double-digit amount. Presently, that person is still at my workplace.

The anger and bitterness that I felt after my employer fired my wife was difficult to deal with. My goal was to re-tell this episode in a novel; not for entertainment, but to encourage every reader to speak out against any subtle or blatant forms of racism in the workplace. If you aren't a worker of color, you can be an ally and stand up for your colleague against any forms of discrimination. Every person, no matter their race or color should be an advocate of anti-racism.

The ending of Part One is intense, and I want to let you know that this story is not about "Black vs White." It's about People vs Racism. God absolutely hates racism, and my goal is to clearly show this in Part Two. Will Jessica and Audre get their jobs back? Who will take the fall for the hate crime on Simon and Tracey? Can Skittles prove that he is innocent of his weapon charge? Will Nezzie's death be too much for Simeon to handle? BRING THE NOISE will address these questions and then some.

In the meantime, if you haven't read my Phat Five series, go to Amazon right now and purchase or download THAT CRAZY WEEKEND pt.1. You won't be disappointed!

Finally, PLEASE PLEASE PLEASE PLEASE PLEASE leave a review of DON'T PUSH ME on Amazon or Goodreads. Do it right now so you won't forget later. Thank you so much! Follow me on Facebook (D.A. Bourne, Author), Instagram (authordabourne), and Twitter (DABourne27). Email me for bookings or inquiries at da.bourne@hotmail.com.

Love and blessings, D.A.

ACTION. COMEDY. DRAMA. BROTHERHOOD. HOPE.
PAPERBACK AND EBOOK AVAILABLE NOW ON
WWW.AMAZON.COM

ABOUT THE AUTHOR

D.A. Bourne is the author of THE PHAT FIVE series. His desire is to bring life and integrity through urban fiction. He was born in Steinbach, Manitoba but has lived in various locations throughout Manitoba, Alberta and Ontario, as well as some time in The Bahamas. D.A currently resides in Brampton, Ontario with his wife and four children. In 1999 D.A received a Bachelor of Arts degree in Communication Studies from the University of Windsor. He entered the publishing world in 2007 and has not stopped writing since. Get ready for more exciting novels by D.A in the very near future.

Manufactured by Amazon.ca
Bolton, ON

18328806R00109